DEDICATION

To my mother, Lucy LeDoux Montoya, who was the inspiration for this particular book and all her Our Fathers and Hail Marys.

Copyright © 2009 Joseph F. Montoya

All rights reserved.

ISBN-10: 1492150029
ISBN-13: 978-1492150022

THE ENDOWMENT

BY

JOSEPH F. MONTOYA
© 2008

CHAPTER 1

" What are you lookin' at?" June Blair inquired of her brother, Delbert. He was staring intently out the kitchen window, trying to see through the rain, which was falling in heavy sheets.

" It's Grace. She's out there doing something," he mumbled, his eyes fixed on his neighbor.

" She oughtn't be out there, not with all that lightning."

" She is though."

The huge willow tree in the Blair front yard was dancing and swaying to the music of the wind, rain and thunder.

" Damned woman's got no sense."

" Now June, she's as smart as they come."

" You're just saying that 'cause--- "

Delbert interrupted her, irritation clear in his voice, " Don't go there June, she's a very smart woman, and you know it. It's got nothin' to do with anything else. You know she's a good woman!"

The thunder was booming overhead like a room full of giant bass drums, and lightning bolts were lighting up the sky.

"What's she doing now?"

" Don't know."

" Can you still see her?"

" Uh-uh," he pressed closer to the window. His eyes flitted back and forth searching for a glimpse of her.

" Get my rain coat and hat, June. I'm going out to look for her."

" I don't know, Delbert. It's too dangerous out there right now."

" June! Go get my rain coat, now!"

June shuffled off and came back with his raincoat and hat.

THE ENDOWMENT

" Are you sure you want to do this?"

" She's our neighbor for God's sake," Del snapped, "and she's all alone. Now get me the good flashlight," he ordered as he put his coat and hat on. He headed for the door, turned back, took his worried sister by the shoulders, and promised softly, "I'll be as careful as I can be sis."

Delbert opened the front door. The wind blasted through, ripped the door from his hand and slammed it into the wall. He caught hold of the edge as it bounced back toward him, struggled with it and closed it, then turned and headed for Grace Jenning's house. It was only about a hundred yards to her front door, but the wind pushed him forward and sideways, then held him back, and the rain slapped his face and clouded his vision.

" Grace," he shouted as lightning lit the sky and thunder cracked with a deafening snap, like a giant bullwhip.

To the left of the road lay the greater expanse of Grace's apple orchard. To the right were the apricots, peaches, prunes, and cherry trees. He couldn't see her from the road, and had no idea where to start looking.

" Grace, can you hear me?" he called again.

The whir of the wind, the pouring fall of the rain and the thunder's almost continuous booming made it impossible to hear anything but nature, roaring its ferocious, inimitable, timeless, terrifying symphony.

Delbert walked past the front door and around the side of the house to get a better view of the corral out back. The light Grace had installed on the high post was out, so it was hard to see anything. The last time he had seen her, she was headed toward the corral, so he pushed forward to the large enclosure. *The barn doors were closed, so the animals were secure,* he thought. He turned and headed back when he saw something on the ground, a person, goat, or a dog, near the corral, about twenty yards away.

The lightning had provided just enough light for him to distinguish there was a something on the ground. He rushed over thinking, it might be Grace's black goat, but as he neared the mound on the ground, it was Grace.

Delbert knelt beside her and saw she was smoldering, like a fire having been put out by rainfall. He could smell singed hair and flesh.

"Grace! Grace! Please, please hear me, Grace," he cried out as he looked up at the heavens.

"Don't let her die. Please, don't let her die," he wailed.

He reached down and scooped her into his arms and ran toward home. When he was near enough, he yelled for June to call the hospital.

She had been watching from the kitchen window and opened the door as he approached. Delbert ran in with Grace's limp, lifeless, body.

"Put her on the couch," she directed. Colt's on his way." She handed him a towel and knelt beside Grace and dried her face with gentle dabs. Her faced looked gnarled. "She's dead, Del," she sobbed.

There was a knock on the door.

"Come in Colt," Delbert called out.

Deputy Colt burst into the room, and took in the scene at a glance.

"It's Grace, Colt. Think a bolt of lightning got her."

"She alive?"

"Don't know. I, I don't think so."

"Where'd it hit her," June asked as she looked down at her.

"Maybe her head, don't know for sure." Delbert croaked.

"Something smells," Colt scowled.

"That's what a bolt of lightning does to ya when it goes through your body. We gotta get her to the hospital, Colt."

"Delbert she's dead!"

"I don't care, gotta get her to the hospital," he said firmly, and picked her up.

"It's pouring shit out there Del, and she's dead."

"Damn it Colt, if you don't drive her, I'll take her myself."

"Del, she's dead," June wailed.

"Open the damned door!"

3

THE ENDOWMENT

Colt opened the door and rushed out in front of Delbert to his patrol car. "Put her in the back seat, Del. You can ride back there with her if you want. June going?"

"Not if she's not out here. Come on, let's move it."

"Do you know what CPR is?" Colt asked looking up at the rear view mirror.

"No."

"Too bad. All right, I'm turning on my lights and siren. Hope the hell we don't kill ourselves."

Delbert moaned softly and whispering to Grace as they sped through the dark, slick rural road.

" Please don't be dead, Grace, please don't die. Please God, don't let her die," he cried shamelessly.

CHAPTER 2

They were racing up Highway 28, racing as fast as the weather would allow.

" How long ago you recken she was struck?" Colt asked in an attempt to engage Delbert's attention. He had been too quiet for several minutes.

" Don't know how long she was layin' out by the corral. Maybe ten minutes since I brought her to the house, just before you got there."

" She was dead then?"

" Well, she wasn't breathin,' at least I couldn't tell that she was 'cause of all the commotion the weather was making."

" She's all that's left of the Jennings, i'nt she, Del?"

"Yup," he uttered through his tears. Delbert was holding her tenderly in his arms, rocking her, as the police car made it's way toward the hospital, with the siren screaming, horn blaring and light flashing.

" Doin' seventy five, Delbert."

" Where are we, Colt?"

" Getting close to the bridge, maybe five minutes."

" She's a good woman,"

" Too bad about her face."

" Never paid any attention to that."

" You know, I never got a call from her for anything. Never, not once."

" She didn't need anyone. Her daddy showed her how to fix things, make things, told her about the apples and cherries. She liked to read too. Read a lotta books, always reading."

" She seemed standoffish, kinda shy, the few times I talked to her."

" She was, on account of her face."

" We're going over the bridge."

" She can't die!" Delbert shouted.

" Ever see a bolt of lighting hit anyone, Del?"

" Yeah, once. Remember Bud Epperson's boy, Tommy?"

" No, don't recken, I do."

THE ENDOWMENT

" Bolt, got him, just a boy."

" That so?"

" We're on Stevens Street now, can't remember, does Okanogan intersect with Stevens?"

" Sure does, turn right on Okanogan, two blocks down and we're at Deaconess."

"Oh yeah, I remember now. Are they expecting us?" Colt asked.

"Should be. I told June to call."

They screeched into the back driveway of the hospital, to the emergency room entrance. There were four white uniforms and hopefully a doctor waiting for the patrol car to stop. A gurney was standing ready. Someone jerked the car door open. Two orderlies and a nurse helped take Grace's limp body out of Del's arms and place it onto a gurney. They quickly disappeared into the hospital. Delbert and Colt followed as far as they were allowed.

A nurse came quietly into the waiting room and gave them each a cup of coffee. A few minutes later a doctor approached.

"You two bring her in?"

"Yes sir," Colt nodded.

"I'm Dr. Biner. How long has she been in this state?"

Colt looked over at Del.

"I guess maybe thirty or thirty five minutes, but it's just a guess, don't know for sure."

"Do you think it was lightning?" he asked Delbert.

"Yes sir, I believe so."

"So, it's maybe close to an hour," he said sadly, mostly to himself, then looked into Del's pleading eyes, "We're doing everything we can. I'll let you know as soon as we know something. I promise."

Colt and Delbert sat silently in the waiting room. Delbert never did like hospitals. They were gloomy, cold and sterile: white walls, cold leatherette chairs and divans, lifeless pictures and the smells of medicines and sickness, and death. Everyone talked in whispers and had long faces. Grace didn't belong here. She was out of place.

" I'm sorry, Grace. I shouldn't have brought you here,"
he said quietly, unaware he was speaking out loud.

" What'd you say, Del?"

" Uh, sorry. Nothing, just talking to myself,"

A woman approached Delbert and Colt.
"I'm Shiela from the admissions office. I'm so sorry about your
friend. I know you're under a lot of stress right now, but we need
some information about her. Who knows her best?"

" I guess I do." Delbert answered miserably.

" Are you a relative?"

" No, ma'am, just a neighbor. She doesn't have family
that I know of."

" Are you certain?"

" Pretty sure. You might have some information on her
birth records. I believe she was born here in this hospital. Grace
J-e-n-n-i-n-g-s. Maybe you could check it out?"

" I certainly will, thank you sir."

CHAPTER 3

In the emergency room a doctor, two nurses and an orderly were quietly cleaning up, pulling forms, and getting ready to move Grace's body. She was still on the gurney after all life saving procedures had been tried. The doctor had checked her vital signs one last time and pronounced her DOA. The medical personnel were quietly going about their duties when--

" I understand," Grace said calmly and clearly as she sat up the white sheet still covering her head. The staff literally dropped what they were doing and gaped at the woman on the gurney. The doctor approached tentatively and pulled down the sheet to expose her face.

" Where am I?" she asked, confusion and near panic clear in her voice as she looked up into his eyes.

He looked down incredulously, "Grace? Oh my God, oh my God, you're alive!"

" Where am I?" she asked again.

" You're, you're in Deaconess Hos-Hospital," he stammered as he grasped a very cold hand.

She wrinkled her forehead, puzzled. "Hospital. Why?"

He looked at the staff. They all stared, open-mouthed, frozen by the shock of having a corpse question what she was doing in their hospital. The doctor knew exactly how they felt.

" It's a miracle," a nurse whispered. Another crossed herself and looked heavenward, her lips moving in prayer, an orderly crossed himself and kneeled.

The doctor put the stethoscope to his ears and listened for a heartbeat. What he heard was a normal rhythm. Well, normal for the circumstances; just a tad on the fast side.

" Let's get an EKG and an EEG," he croaked. "I'm going to give her a thorough exam. After, I'd like a blood work up. Mary help me with the examination." OK people, let's move!"

Shiela, from the office, came running back into the visiting room.

8

" She's alive! Grace is alive!" The poor woman was beside herself, and could think of nothing else to say. " She's alive!"

Delbert and Colt were struck dumb and immobile at the pronouncement. When the information finally made its way to the working part of their brains, in unison they screamed, "Grace!" jumped up, embraced each other, and pulled Shiela into their hug then danced around the waiting room like crazy men.

Tears were streaming down Delbert's face again. " I can't remember the last time I cried so damned much. Shiela, you're sure, aren't you?"

"Sure as the sun rising. She's alive," she hugged them again, and left the waiting room like she was floating on clouds.

At that moment a very solemn June walked slowly into the visitors room.

" She's alive, June! Grace is alive!"

" But, but, how can that be?"

" It's a damned miracle. I mean it's a great miracle. She's alive, she's alive." He picked up his sister and whirled her around and around in the air.

" Delbert you big ox, put me down before you kill me," she squealed.

Nurse Harris approached the trio, her eyes were still red and teary, but her expression was beatific. "Doctor is giving Grace a VERY thorough checkup. You *migh*t be able to see her in about an hour and a half. I'm so excited I'm not thinking clearly. What happened in there is a miracle, a real, honest to God, miracle," she squeezed Del's arm and returned to the examining room.

Colt, choking back tears, approached the others, "I gotta get back, Del. Glad you're here June. Sure would like to hang around a while, but things are still crazy out there. My dispatcher is giving me all kinds of grief," he grinned.

" Thanks, Colt. You prob'ly saved her life."

" I think it's you we'd better thank, Del. You're the one with the ants in your pants about getting her to the hospital." Colt became quiet and solemn, "Del, I believe, well, damn it,

THE ENDOWMENT

this is hard to say out loud, but, I agree with that nurse. I believe we saw a miracle tonight. That's all it could be, a miracle."

They shook hands and Colt left.

" Wow, all of sudden, I'm hungry June."

" I believe there's a canteen downstairs."

They walked downstairs and found some vending machines. As they munched on chips and cookies, Del spoke queitly, " You know June, I held her all the way to the hospital. That's as close as I ever been with her. She's really beautiful."

" You've always favored her. "

Del nodded.

They sat and drank their coffee in silence. It had been quite an evening all right. Not one would easily forget.

Shiela came into the room and approached Del, "Sir, the doctor wants to see you when you get through eating. He thought you had gone home."

He stood. " I'm ready now."

They walked up the stairs and she directed him to the waiting room.

Delbert sat and waited. He felt calm for the first time in several hours.

" Hello, it's me again, I didn't get your name earlier."

" Delbert Blair."

" Well, Mr. Blair, do you believe in miracles."

Delbert nodded and smiled. " She's always been a special person."

" You're her neighbor?"

" Yes sir."

" Well, there is no other word for what transpired here this evening. We were just discussing taking her down to the morgue, and she spoke from under the sheet. Just like she was speaking to someone in the room. We *knew* she was dead, but it's hard to believe that now, since I've just examined her thoroughly, and I couldn't find anything, not one thing, wrong with her. Her hair is singed and she has holes in her shoes where the lightning passed through. Is she a Christian lady?

Delbert looked down at the floor, then up at the doctor. " Well, we've never discussed it, but I certainly believe she has Christian ways about her."

"What exactly did she say from under the sheet. Doctor?"

Doctor Biner hesitated, clearly uncomfortable, then looked Del in the eyes and almost whispered. "She said, 'I understand.'"

Del thought about the words. " Strange. I'm gonna try to remember to ask her about it later. Thanks."

The doctor hesitated a moment then ventured, "Del, she's an attractive woman, do you know why she never had that nevus removed as a youngster?"

" Nevus?"

"Nevus, the birthmark on her face."

" I don't know anything about that."

" Well, we're going to run a few more tests and maybe we can let her go home in a couple of days."

"Thank you, Doctor. Um, can I see her?"

"I'm sorry, not tonight. Why don't you call in the morning? We'll know more by then."

June walked up as the doctor was leaving. "Does she get to go home, Del?"

" They're going to keep her for a couple of days, run some tests, and we *can't* see her tonight. I'm really tired June. Let's go home."

11

CHAPTER 4

The storm had subsided to a few small gray clouds and a wet highway. The ride back to Palisades was quiet. There was little traffic and Delbert was staring out the window at the mighty Columbia River, almost as if in a trance. He was tired. The last few hours had been a nightmare, but had, miraculously, turned out OK.

" What do you think happened, Del?" June ventured.

" God only knows. The doctor called it a miracle. I don't know what else it could be."

" I swear she was dead when you brought her to the house."

" I know. She was dead out by the corral; she was dead on the ride to the hospital; she was dead when they took her into the Emergency Room. Then she just…woke up."

June pulled into their driveway and parked. The storm had bandied things around on their small ranch and now it was eerily quiet. They parked in front of Graces house in silence.

"Maybe you should go check on her animals, Del. See if they've been fed. I'll check inside the house."

June was aware Grace had birds. Grace's parrots, an African Gray and a Blue-fronted Amazon, watched her calmly as she approached. She found food under their metal cages, filled their dishes with seeds, and gave them fresh water. They promptly dove in and threw seeds everywhere as they searched for their favorite morsels. The sweet tempered dogs, Mandy and Daisy, slowly wagged their way to her, the familiar neighbor, as if to ask where Grace was. Their soft, dark eyes seemed to overflow with grief and sadness. She comforted them in a gentle tone with news about Grace. June could swear they understood what she had said. They looked almost relieved. "Good grief, you silly woman! They can't understand you!" she admonished herself. But still…

As she looked around the neatly furnished home, she realized she had never been in the front room, and felt almost guilty. Grace had an eye for furniture and knick-knacks. How

12

could they have lived so close for such a long time, and remained so far apart? But she knew why. Grace was an intensely private person, And, she supposed, she wasn't much different.

" June, everything all right in there?" Del called from the doorway.

" Yeah, I think so."

"You know, Del, I just realized I've never been in here. Her daddy left her a mighty nice place." She mused as she approached the front door. " I'm not going to lock the door, unless you know where Grace might keep a key. The corral all right?"

" They have plenty of hay and oats out there. I'll come back in the morning and let 'em into the corral."

CHAPTER 5

It was three days later when the hospital called the Blairs to come and take Grace home.

"Thank you, Delbert, I didn't know anyone else to call."

"Well then, I'm glad you called me. You look great, certainly better than the last time I saw you."

"The doctor told me you and the deputy brought me here. Sorry to have put you through all that. I guess from now on, I'm going to consider you my guardian angel," she said, smiling shyly.

Delbert blushed, " You're probably anxious to get home, and I know some critters who, I swear, know you're coming today."

"Often thought those guys could read my mind." She said quietly.

On their drive home the scenery held her attention. It had never been more beautiful. She turned to gaze solemnly at Delbert.

"I guess I'm lucky to be able to see the river flowing, and the trees, and this beautiful day."

"I don't know if I'd call it luck. The doctor said it was a miracle, and I believe it was."

"I don't remember anything after I walked out of the house and headed for the corral; nothing, till I opened my eyes to find a nurse asking me if I wanted dinner. She told me I'd been there for two days."

" Well, it's pretty hard to tell you now, that I believed you were dead, then."

" The lightning?"

" Yup, I didn't see it hit you, but I believe it hit your head and went down through your shoes. Your hair was singed and you were still smoldering when I reached you. You weren't breathing. Don't know how long you laid there before I reached you," his voice was husky with the effort to keep sorrow from coming through.

" Must have been ghastly. I'm so sorry, Delbert," as she gently touched his shoulder.

" June and I have been in and out of your house while you been gone, Grace. We felt it was necessary, hope you don't take offense."

" Like I said, Delbert, my guardian angel has been on duty and working for me this whole time and I thank you, thank you, thank you."

As she stepped from the car she took a deep breath and marveled in the treasured scents of her own special place, her home.

" It's sure good to be home."

After she had greeted, and been greeted by, all the critters, and Del had gotten her settled in and comfortable, Grace insisted he 'get on with his business'. Reluctantly he headed out, "Holler if you need anything," he called and drove down to the corral to turn around.

As he came back by, she waved and he stopped.

" Someone from the Daily World is coming to see me, Delbert. Just wanted you and June to know."

" The Newspaper?"

" Yep, the Wenatchee Daily World is coming to see me. Seems some one at the hospital thought what happened is news, and called them. I declined at first, but the reporter's a woman and she thinks a positive, human-interest story would be a good thing. No pictures, of course. I think it'll be all right, Delbert."

CHAPTER 6

As Del drove up the long driveway he was thinking
about the lady who was coming to talk to her. Grace was a very
smart woman and could hold her own with anyone. She was
always polite, no matter what the provocation; but damn it, she
was so innocent! What was he getting all riled up for? "If Grace
wanted to talk to some newspaper reporter, that was her
business," he said out loud.

He walked into the house still grumbling.

"How does she look?" June asked Del as she came from
the kitchen.

" Oh, she looks fine. There' a lady reporter coming to
talk to her."

" Is that what the long face is for?"

" She's a private person. You know that. I'm a little
concerned about the kind of publicity she might get from this.
I'm not sure she understands what could happen."

" Publicity?"

" Yes June, *publicity*! That reporter is going to write
something about Grace in the Wenatchee Daily World. Heaven
knows what she'll say, and a lot of people are going to read it,"
he fussed.

" Why does that bother you so much?"

" Well, I'm probably out of line saying this, but the crack
pots might start coming out of the woodwork. She doesn't need
that!"

"Do you think they will put her address in the paper?"

"I don't know, but they might say she's from Palisades,
and everybody knows Palisade's just a blip on the road. If they
come looking, they'll find her for sure."

CHAPTER 7

A week later, the article appeared in the paper. The reporter had not only interviewed Grace, but every person she could find who had been at the hospital that night, as well. It was all there.

Grace Jennings, of Palisades, had been struck by a bolt of lightning that had gone through her, entering at the top of her head and burning straight down through her feet. Sheriff's Deputy Colt, and her neighbor, Delbert Blair, had rushed her to the hospital through the storm, which was battering the area at that time. Neither Deputy Colt nor Delbert Blair was interviewed. The Deputy was out of state, and the reporter had not yet located Mr. Blair.

The staff at Deconess Hospital all agreed that Grace was DOA, but that the Emergency Room staff had nevertheless performed every life-saving procedure, before the doctor had pronounced her dead. As the ER team was cleaning up and getting ready to roll the gurney out, Grace had spoken! Scared everyone half to death. She was alive! Not only alive, but, after several days of testing and examination, it was determined she was perfectly healthy, as though nothing had ever happened to her.

THE ENDOWMENT

CHAPTER 8

Twenty-nine days later.

There was a frantic banging on the Blairs's front door. Delbert had just settled down to pay some bills. Not one of his favorite chores. The interruption was just one more irritation and he was tempted to ignore whoever it was. As he scowled at the door, muttering under his breath, the pounding became one of those, 'LET ME IN NOW' knocks. He stood, took off his glasses and turned to the door just as someone pounded again, even more emphatically. He jerked the door open, ready to give the intruder a piece of his mind, but pulled up short, surprised to find, a somewhat frantic, Grace. His ire instantly flipped to worry.

"Are you all right?" as he grasped her shoulders, pulled her into the house, and checked outside to see if he could see what had panicked the relatively unflappable woman.

"Delbert? Delbert? I, uh, I...oh my God!" Grace couldn't put together the right words, and the look in her eyes pleaded with him. But to do what?

He would do it! Whatever it was. Just as soon as she told him what it was, it was done! Then it hit him!

"It was that reporter lady, wasn't it? What she put in the paper. I knew she was trouble from the minute I-"

"No, no," was all Grace could manage to voice as she slowly wagged her head negatively.

"Grace? Oh my God, Grace! Is everything all right?" June asked as she took in the scenerio in her living room and rushed to her side.

"Would you like something to drink? Maybe a glass of water?" Delbert offered, almost frantic to do something, anything to make Grace OK again.

She took a deep breath, closed her eyes, and dropped her chin to her chest.

"I'm embarrassed, I shouldn't have come, shouldn't have bothered you."

18

"Whatever it is, it can't possibly be as bad as what's running through Del's mind right now. You'd best calm down, and tell us before he takes off looking for somebody to whup," June advised semi-seriously.

Grace sat in silence on the frayed cushioned chair kneading her left palm with her right thumb for a long minute, finally looking up at Delbert and June.

"I really don't know how to say this, it sound so preposterous. Grace slumped, took a deep breath, and tried again. "I was out early this morning, checking the irrigation ditches under the apple trees. As I was walking along the ditch, I practically stepped on this sweet, little, gentle faced dove. Poor thing appeared to have a broken wing. She tried to get out of harm's way, and fluttered away awkwardly on one wing. I walked over to her and she allowed me to pick her up. I could see where her wing was broken. There was blood and I could see the bone break on the wing. I put my hands around her to hold her wings, you know, to keep them from flapping and started to the house. When I got to the house and had to use one hand to open the door, she just flew to a nearby cherry tree and looked down at me, then flew away. I was left standing there with my mouth wide open!"

"Are you sure her wing was broken?"

"Unless I'm going blind, that wing was broken."

The three sat, quietly, contemplating what Grace had said. How could that dove have been able to fly away? Then Grace roused from her confused thoughts, smiled, and announced quietly, "I healed a dove! I healed a dove!"

Neither June nor Delbert could speak. All three were frozen in the moment. Slowly Delbert started to grin, then grew to laughter. June joined in, and then Grace. The laughter gradually subsided and finally quiet. Delbert returned to his chair, sat, and faced Grace and queried her solemnly, "You healed a dove?"

She nodded.

"How could that be?" June asked.

Delbert ventured, "About the only thing that makes any sense, Grace, is that the wing *wasn't* broken."

"Delbert, the wing *was* broken! I'm sure of it."

THE ENDOWMENT

"Have you ever done anything like this before?" Delbert asked.

She shook her head, "You two are my neighbors and my closest friends. If this had happened before, you would have heard about it! This is as new to me as it is to you.

"Maybe, we should forget the whole thing. Just pretend it never happened, otherwise, I don't know what to do." Del stated flatly.

"Well, I don't know if we can forget something like this, but I'd be careful who I mention it to, Grace. For my part, I don't plan to tell a soul!"

Grace stood and moved slowly toward the door, "You're still going to be my friends, aren't you... even though I might be losing my mind?"

"Honey, if you're losing your mind, we're in it together, 'cause we believe what you told us. Just don't understand it, but then, they're a lot of things we don't understand. Maybe we're not supposed to." She put her arm around her friend and kissed her on the cheek. You're *not* crazy! We love you, Grace, don't we Delbert?"

Delbert, suddenly tongue-tied and flushed, walked into the kitchen without answering.

" He loves you Grace, take my word for it. He's just too shy to say so."

20

CHAPTER 9

A month later - May 1956

Delbert was repairing a ladder in the small barn behind his house when he heard Grace calling his name.

"I'm in the barn."

Grace blew into the barn like a whirlwind, grabbed his arm and tugged him toward the door. "Delbert, come over to my house, right away. June too."

"June's not here, but I'll come with you, if you don't pull my arm off," he teased.

"Sorry," she mumbled, wrapped her arm under his and continued to tug him toward her house."

He blushed. "So what's the emergency?"

"I'll tell you when we get there, I promise. There's a woman, with a small girl, and, I'll let her tell you."

They entered the front room and he saw a woman sitting on the sofa beside a small girl wearing a black watch cap. The woman stood when she saw them.

"Hello, sir. My name is Joan Demmek, and this is my daughter, Sandra. The minute I told Miss Jennings why I had come, she insisted that you and your sister be here."

"Why *are* you here?"

"Well, it's a long story, but I'll try to be brief.

"We, my family, are Russian. My grandfather and grandmother came to America in the early 1900's and settled in Washington State. They had heard it was a lot like where our family had come from; a small town, close to Kiev, Cherkasy. Maybe you heard of it? Anyway, my grandfather told my mother a story about a young woman walking home from another small village who had been struck by lightning, and she lived. Shortly after, she began to heal people. God had given her the power," she looked up at Delbert from under her bangs, and slowly sat down.

"Oh, and you think Grace here, might have this power, this God given power? " What I can tell you is that Grace is a wonderful woman, law abiding, honest, trustworthy, hard working, kind, and beautiful too, but she does not attend any

21

THE ENDOWMENT

Christian church. I'm not sure she even believes in God.
Forgive me Grace, I - I'm talking out of turn and I'm probably
all wet."

Grace touched his arm and smiled reassuringly, "Delbert,
you know me better than I thought."

" Well, Mr. Delbert, if God chooses you, you do not have
the choice to turn Him down. Besides, my desperation is great. I
am praying that Miss Jennings has the power. My daughter's life
depends on that belief. If she doesn't, then my daughter will be
in heaven before me," her voice trembled and caught. When she
could speak again, she did so earnestly, "My family believes in
miracles. I believe in miracles. Please, sir. We've come a long
way. Please let her try. I beg you!" she pleaded.

"Ma'am. Ma'am, please don't cry. I have nothing to say
about what Grace does or doesn't do. I'm only her friend and
have her best interests at heart."

Grace, who had been standing by the front door listening
to the conversation, approached the sobbing woman and the
frightened child. "Honestly Joan, I haven't the slightest idea how
to go about doing anything like healing your daughter. But, God
knows, I would if I knew how---"

Joan took a deep breath, composed herself and looked
into Grace's worried eyes.

"The story goes that the young woman would put her
hands on the person that was to be healed," Joan said solemnly.

"And if I do that, and it doesn't work?"

"Then, beautiful Grace, I will thank you for trying and I
will pray for you, and be grateful that you tried. You may be my
last ray of hope. I would have driven a thousand miles for this
opportunity. I will be forever in your debt, whatever happens."

Grace, tears in her eyes, turned slowly to little Sandra
and looked into her pale, listless, hollow, blue eyes.

"May I remove your cap sweetheart?" Sandra said
nothing, just gazed trustingly at Grace as she removed the cap to
reveal the shaved head, bisected by a large angry scar.

Grace delicately placed her hands on Sandra's head and
closed her eyes. Several seconds later, a tremor rolled like an
earthquake through her body and out through her hands. When

the "quake" had passed Grace was thrown backward, where, by pure happenstance, Delbert caught her. Sandra collapsed.

Grace was strangely calm, as if in a trance. When her senses returned and she saw Sandra she cried out, "Oh my God, I've killed her." She scrambled over to the tiny, fragile, motionless little girl. "What have I done? Delbert, I've killed this poor innocent child," she sobbed. She stood and turned away with Delbert's assistance walked toward the window. He was trying to console her, as she sobbed and berated herself.

"Miss Grace, Miss Grace," a soft, tiny voice broke through to her consciousness when she felt a tug on her hand, "Miss Grace."

Delbert and Grace slowly turned and looked down into a beautifully radiant, smiling, face. Grace knelt and pulled the child into her arms and hugged her tightly as tears spilled down her cheeks.

"I feel better, Miss Grace. Thank you."

She looked over Sandra's head at Joan, then fainted dead away.

Delbert picked her up and carried her to the sofa. When she opened her eyes she was looking at three, very worried, faces.

"I fainted…I'm sorry," she stammered as she tried to sit up. Sandy, the worry draining from her little face, ran to her and hugged her as she lay on the sofa. Grace could feel the strength in her arms, and the warmth of her tears as they trickled down her neck. Grace sat up. Joan came, sat beside them and joined the group hug.

Delbert, who was deeply touched by what he had seen, opened the door, stepped outside, and looked at the trees in the orchard.

"Delbert, come back inside, please," Grace beckoned.

Inside, the four stood in silence until Grace asked earnestly, "Do you honestly feel better, Sandy?"

"I do. I think I'm better!"

"Well," she sighed and more composed, " I have to admit, ever since the Dove flew out of my hands, I thought there might be something different, something special happening, if it is true? Why? And why me?"

THE ENDOWMENT

Joan knelt down in front of Grace, crossed herself and started to pray.

"Please, Joan, please don't do that. I'm not special. Something special may have happened to me, but I'm certainly not special, and we still don't know for sure if Sandy is cured…healed, really."

"You have been endowed with a special gift from God," Joan whispered reverently."

"I can't believe this-this, was meant for me. Do you Delbert?"

Nothing from Delbert, he still looked like *he* had just been struck by lightening.

"The young woman my mother told me about was from a poor family and was of no consequence to the villagers." Joan spoke softly, "She was a nobody. But God chose her for a reason, His own reason. We could only guess what it may have been. Why you? Again, we can only guess, but I don't believe God made a mistake."

The room became quiet.

"So, now what do I do?"

"You will know what to do, when he wants you to know," Joan said solemnly.

"There is no way to repay you for what you have done, but only say the word and I will try. My daughter owes her life to you and to God. I will stay for as long as you want, Miss Grace. For now, I will fix your lunch if you so desire. You are probably famished.

"No Joan, you owe me nothing. I believe I am just an instrument, although, a very confused one." Grace leaned down, picked Sandra up, hugged her affectionately and kissed her on the cheek. I love you sweetie, and hope you have a wonderful life. You're a beautiful girl." She set her down and hugged Joan." Now you must go."

"God has blessed you, Grace." They held on to each other for a long minute and when they stepped apart Joan and Sandy quietly departed.

"Let me fix you lunch, Delbert. Please. I need to do something with my hands right now, and I think I owe you a meal."

24

"I don't think you do, but I'll take you up on the offer anyway."

She made a pot of coffee, poured him a cup and started to fry a steak.

They sat at the table and tried to eat, but ended up pushing the food around on their plates.

"That Joan seemed to be completely sold on the story her mother passed on to her," Del ventured tentatively.

"I would say Joan's a good Christian woman and firmly believes God works in strange ways," she said as she slathered butter on a slice of bread. "Delbert, you haven't said anything about what happened here today."

"I don't know if I'm dreaming, or if I'm in your dream or what, but so far none of this makes any sense. I keep thinking I'm going wake up any minute."

"I'm not sure I did anything but make little Sandy feel better. "That awful scar was still on her head."

He nodded, "saw that."

THE ENDOWMENT

CHAPTER 10

A week later

"Miss Jennings, this is Joan Demmek. I just arrived home from the doctor's office in Seattle.

I believed when Sandy and I left your house she had been cured. But that's what I *wanted* to believe, because she's my daughter and I had no choice. I wasn't brave enough to believe anything else.

"But you, well, this was your first miracle. I felt you had doubts and that's understandable. Now, I'm confirming to you that my doctor called it a miracle, 'for the lack of a better word.' That's what he said, 'for the lack of a better word.' I want you to know that I told him it was the *appropriate* word."

"Oh my gosh, what wonderful news, Joan," Grace stammered.

"Grace you will always be in my prayers and of course, if you ever need me, for anything, please call. Now that I've said those words, they sound absurd. What could I possibly do for you? Anyway, call me if you need me."

Grace ambled up the road from her house to the Blair's home and stepped up on the small porch.

"Come on in, Grace." June called out from the kitchen window.

She stepped in dejectedly.

"You look a little down. Are you all right?"

"You remember the woman and the little girl that came to my house a week ago?"

"I wasn't here that day, but Delbert told me about them, what about them?"

"Well, she just called. "

Delbert, drifted into the kitchen covered in dust from the barn.

"Hi, Delbert. I was just telling June, that Joan Demmek called about her daughter.

"Is she all right?" he asked walking to the sink to wash.

26

"The doctor that was treating her in Seattle, called it a miracle. What am I going to do June, Delbert? This scares me."

"Maybe we're making too much of all this, honey. Didn't you feel good about little Sandy? How about the dove? It seems to me you might be able to make a lot of very unfortunate people feel good. Is that so bad?"

"What about all the kooks that are going crawl out of the woodwork, the ones that'll try to take advantage of her. The crazies, the schemers, scammers, the derelicts, the greedy, what about them?" Delbert steamed as his voice raised an octave.

"What about them?" June asked. "They're always around, and Grace is no dummy. Isn't that right, Gracie?"

"You're right June, I've been feeling sorry for myself, only looking at the down side. My father left me more money than I could ever spend. I have a nice home, an orchard, two fantastic horses, two wonderful dogs, goats, two parrots, two sheep a few chickens and a myriad of wild crows, doves, blue Jays, a skunk that lives somewhere close by and some wild rabbits. How much more blessed could I be? I guess it's my turn to give a little back. As Joan said, maybe I've been chosen by God to heal, and heal I will, and hope I can sustain what I'm feeling now, always."

CHAPTER 11

Grace spent the next few weeks on her little farm watering her orchard and examining and tightening all her wooden ladders. The cherry season, June and July, and then the apple season in late fall would be here before she knew it. The years seemed to be getting shorter and shorter.

The future had her a little spooked. Not knowing what might be on the horizon, she determined it would be prudent to get everything in order, besides, she was buzzing with nervous energy.

She fixed the minor damage the storm had done to the roof of her house and the barn, changed the oil in her Ford tractor and had new tires put on her old trailer, the one that was used for bringing cherries and apples out of the orchard.

She took a couple of days off and went to Lake Chelan and her cabin.

She changed the three or four damaged fence posts along the road to the house, visited with June and Delbert and the Robertson's, the neighbors that lived further down the road.

Grace loved the warm sunny mornings, cloudless sky, the sweet smell of hay, clover, and the roses she had planted along the side of her house. She had a load of new hay delivered for the penned animals and painted the barn a Lambert cherry red.

All this activity had been precipitated by the fact that she didn't know where her new power would take her, a power she did not ask for, but now felt compelled to utilize.

A month had passed and one morning she woke up, stretched, and knew it was time. She was ready to be shown the way. She fed her little menagerie, cleaned up and strolled over to the Blair's place to inform them that if God called on her she was ready and would be off to do his bidding, and to ask if they would be kind enough to help her foreman run the farm.

How would she know when he was ready to put her to work? Her thoughts went back to that stormy, angry evening, the night of the storm and lightning. She smiled wryly to herself.

28

What a strange way to ask someone to heal? No offense, God, but, a bolt through the head? And why me, I can think of a lot of other people more qualified than me. Father O'Sullivan or Father Duffy came to mind. How about Pastor Price from the Presbyterian Church or the lady who used to spend all her money on Bibles and then stand on the corner of Wenatchee Avenue and Orondo Street and give them away? I always thought she was pretty special...wonder what ever happed to her? How about Tracy Truman's girl-scout leader? She made cookies and cakes for her troops, marched up the face of Saddle Rock; took them fishing to Twin Lakes and bought some of them fishing poles. She even went to the slaughterhouse at the North end and shoveled up the big angleworms. Those were the big ones, sure to catch fish. You know God, I'm not trying to make light of this, to be irreverent, but it's a complete mystery why you chose me.

Another week passed.

"Sorry to interrupt your breakfast Delbert, June, but I'm going to drive to Omak tomorrow. Just wanted you to know I haven't run off. Jimmy's going to take care of the place, so don't worry.

"Can I be nosey?" June asked.

"Joan Demmek wants me to talk to someone up there and see if I can do them some good."

"Would you like some company?"

"I sure would Delbert. I would have asked you but you've already done so much for me and I didn't feel right about it. It's always nice to someone like you around. Would you mind, June?"

"Honey, Delbert has a mind of his own, besides our foreman is here now."

CHAPTER 12

The next morning Grace and Delbert set off in her green and white 1956 Buick Special along Highway 28, following the Columbia River, crossing the river on the south end of Wenatchee and heading northeast on Highway 97.

"How about breakfast?" she asked.

"It's still a little early for me. Maybe Entiat or Chelan, unless you're hungry."

"Not really, Entiat's fine."

"Heard they were going to put up a dam by Entiat."

"That'd be good, maybe it would stop the flooding problem they had in Wenatchee in '48. Remember that?"

"Read about it in the Daily World," He responded.

"Didn't you date Susan Harmony a few years ago?"

"I did."

"She was so pretty."

"Yes she was."

"No fire?"

"I guess not, besides, she wanted to go to the University."

"She sure was crazy about you."

"I don't know about that. What makes you say that?"

"I just heard it somewhere."

Grace thought, *he's so shy and handsome, yet there is something mysterious about him. Maybe he doesn't really like girls, because if Susan couldn't light a fire under him, I can't imagine who could, and he's trying to avoid the subject. Oh well – it's his business.* " Do you and June still have a cabin in 25 Mile Creek?"

He nodded.

" Why didn't you get---"

After the tunnel the highway had been slowly up. They reached the top and were now descending into west Lake Chelan.

30

"There she is, our beautiful 50 mile lake," she remarked." After an uneasy silence she answered his half finished question.

"Oh, I was almost in love once."

"Thomas Crumb!" he remarked.

"Why, yes, it was Thomas Crumb. I wasn't aware you knew who he was."

"I knew he was smart."

"Actually, that's what came between us. He wanted to be doctor and I've always wanted to be just what I am, a farmer. Can you see me living in a city? I've always loved where I am, never wanted to be anywhere else; just your typical homely, little 4H, farm girl."

"You're not homely."

"You're sweet. Thank you. Don't you think it's strange that we live less than a hundred yards apart and we really don't know each other. I'm not sure our parents knew each other that well, either."

He nodded in agreement.

"Time goes fast with good company, we've arrived in Omak. Joan told me to give her a call when got here, so I'll pull into the first gas station I see and call from there. Might as well fill her up with gas, too. Oh good, there's a Chevron Station." She stopped, slowly crawled out of the vehicle and moaned as she stretched out her back and leg muscles.

"Good afternoon, ma'am. Fill 'er up with Premium?" the attendant inquired, as he strode to her side.

"Regular will be fine."

"Should be using Premium, ma'am, takes the ping out of those valves."

"Think so?"

"Yes ma'am,"

"All right, fill her up with Premium."

"Can I check the water and oil for you ma'am?"

"Please." After walking around a little, getting the circulation back in her legs, she strolled over to the pay phone.

The attendant came over to the passenger side and asked Delbert if he could trouble him to step out of the car so he could sweep his side of the floor-board: empty the ash tray and discard

THE ENDOWMENT

any trash from the car. Grace returned, reiterating the directions Joan had given her over in her mind. The attendant approached her and showed her the dipstick. She didn't need oil. He closed the hood, wiped the windshields, topped off her gas.

"Your gas tank took just a shade over ten gallons and that will be $3.76 cents. Will you be paying with your Chevron card or cash, ma'am?" She handed him a $5,00 bill. He ran off and came back with her change, "By the way ma'am, your tires were at 32 pounds, which is right where they should be. Have a nice trip."

"Thank you."

Grace drove slowly through the small town of Omak, took Alma road right for a mile, left on Douglas Fur for a little over half-mile to Seattle Road. She was looking for a white house on the right side that needed painting, with a blue 1937 four door Chevrolet parked in front.

"I think that's Joan Demmek I see, up ahead on the right." She drove into the short drive way and stopped as Joan came walking over. "Thank you for coming, Miss Jennings," she said stepping aside and letting Grace out of her car. Delbert exited too.

"Hi Delbert, nice to see you, she added. I was hoping you would accompany her up here, it's a long trip by herself, thank you."

He nodded.

"Sara Thompson is the woman you're going to see and she's inside right now. We're waiting for her brother, Bill Stanfield, and he should be here in a few minutes. I called him just after you called me, Miss Grace. I haven't told anyone you made my daughter well. Bill Stanfield doesn't know. He's hesitant about someone coming over here to see his sister when she's in such a bad state. Hope you understand. His language might be coarse, I apologize now, for anything he might say to you inappropriately. Please be tolerant. I believe that's him coming down the road now.

Bill Stanfield stepped up to the three that were waiting for him. He was somber and wore his skepticism openly. His blue eyes flashed suspiciously. Clad in a pair of faded coveralls,

32

scuffed work shoes, and a blue denim shirt, he looked every bit the red neck.

"Bill this is Grace Jennings and Delbert Blair, they're here to see your sister."

He peered at Grace dubiously. She was wearing a one-piece cotton, light blue dress with a thin black belt, and a light summer button down sweater and a pair of black Mary Jane shoes. "Are you an evangelist?" he asked cynically. "What's that on your face?"

Delbert, who had been leaning on Grace's car, stood straight up. "I don't think that-"

"It's all right, Delbert, Grace interjected. Mr. Stanfield, the red on my face is a birthmark. I'm not a doctor. I'm no one special. I'm just a friend of Joan and her daughter. She invited me to come and see your sister and possibly talk to her. I would like your approval to do just that. I'm not going to hurt her in any way, I assure you. I don't blame you for your skepticism. You have every right to feel that way. I'm sure I would feel the same way. However, if you disapprove, Delbert and I will turn around and leave."

"Bill, they drove all the way from Palisades to see Sara," Joan beseeched.

Mr. Stanfield studied the ground for a few seconds, "that's a long way, I don't suppose it would hurt to go inside and talk to her."

"Can't get her to eat nothin', won't say nothin', jest lays there. Doctor don't know what to make of it. Says he cain't find nothing could make her like that. You're wastin' your time, I'm tellin' ya. But if you're set on seein' her...go on ahead."

"Thank you sir," Grace said politely.

Bill Stanfield led the way, opening a door that needed paint years ago. They followed him into a small front room that had an old treadle Singer sewing machine by the door. Immediately, to the right was the oldest couch Grace had ever seen, with the springs visible through the seat covers, the cushions frayed, the arms showing the wood skeleton. It belonged in the dump. The floor to Sara's bedroom creaked as they crossed the room, and was in desperate need of repair. She was lying in a bed that swayed like an old horse's back. There

33

THE ENDOWMENT

were only thin blankets over the ancient springs for a mattress.
Above her head on the wall was a lone, simple cross. The rest of
the room was devoid of anything, except for a stand-up lamp
with no bulb.

"Can I get you a stool to sit on?" Bill Stanfield, asked
quietly.   "I'll just kneel, thank you."

Grace knelt beside the poor woman and began to cry.
Why would she want to save this woman to this dreadful life of
despair?

Delbert, standing by the door, was taking all this in and
was feeling the empathy Grace displayed for the woman on the
bed. Joan entered the room quietly and stood by Delbert, both
staring at the pathetic scene.

Grace suddenly stood, turned and walked to the two of
them.

"I can't do this Joan. Look at this house, look how she
lives. I'm not doing this woman any good. I can't do it. She's
better off dead. Where's the rest of her family, don't they care? I
can't believe this whole scene. What am I doing here, this is
crazy. Keep her alive for what? This is abject poverty;
hopelessness, misery, despair. Why would a just and good God
want this woman to live like this? Tell me Joan, Why?"

Joan stared into Grace's eyes for a moment. "I don't have
an answer for you Miss Grace, but yours is not to question why.
You have been chosen. Would you dare defy God?"

"I don't know what I dare to do at this point."

She looked over at Delbert and felt shame. Tears welled
in her eyes and she opened her arms. Delbert came to her and
held her.

Grace slowly calmed, then turned and knelt by the bed
and grasped Sara Thompson by the shoulders. Grace shook
violently and then tremors ran through hands and straight to
Sara's body. The bed squeaked and rattled and hit the wall and
the cross fell on Sara's chest. Grace sat back on her feet and
leaned forward. She was tired.

"Who are you?" a soft voice asked.

Grace looked at the tired face, "My name is Grace, and
you're Sara."

"Do I know you?"

"You may regret having met me."

"Pardon me."

Sara looked across the room at Joan and stood precariously. She walked unreliably to her and hugged her. "I know you," then, realizing she was standing in her robe, she shuffled out of the room.

Joan walked over to Grace and helped her stand and hugged her tightly.

"You did good."

"I hope you're right,"

"I know I'm right and I know you will eventually know that you are right in what you are doing."

"Joan, we've got to be going, try not to say too much about me. OK? You do understand?"

"By the way, how old is Sara? And where is all her family?"

Joan took her by the hand and tugged her to the back window. She pulled back the ragged curtain just an inch and Grace peeked out and there, in the yard, stood about 30 or 35 people.

"What are they doing out there?"

"They were waiting for a miracle and they got one, you silly girl." She grabbed Grace and kissed her just as Sara walked back into the room. "Grace has to go, Sara. I'm going to walk her to her car and I'll be right back."

"Where is everybody, Joan?"

"They're waiting for you out behind the house."

"It was nice to meet you-"

"Grace. Good luck to you, Sara, come, give me a hug."

Grace and Joan walked outside arm in arm.

"I thought you might be out here waiting for me. Did you know that Delbert was my guardian angel?"

"Please Delbert, take good care of our sweet Doubting Thomasina. Oh, yes, she's forty-six. Sara's age."

"Thank you." She said as she backed out of the driveway.

"Who is that woman, Joan?" Sara asked bewildered.

"Oh, just a friend." She said with a wry smile.

THE ENDOWMENT

Grace and Delbert made their way out of Omak and were now driving down 97.

"I'm having a tuff time handling this thing Delbert. Maybe it takes time to adjust to helping people. What do you think?"

"I don't know, I can't imagine me doing what your doing. Honestly, I don't believe I could do it. We were pretty much on the same page back there at Sara's house.

"I'm glad Joan was there. You know, she's right about what she said. You know, the 'I'm not to question why?' thing. But, I'm not some robot, I'm, I've got feelings. Everything I saw in that house, screamed at me to let her go to a better place. Oh my God, how dare I play God, deciding who should live and who should die. I think that's what I was doing, Delbert, playing God." She began crying. "Doesn't it seem like I'm always crying now?"

"Would you like me to drive, Grace?"

"Would you?" she said, as she slowed the car and pulled off the road.

Delbert drove for several miles and Grace just observed the peaceful milieu of sagebrush and the occasional clump of pine trees.

"We're becoming quite the duo, you and me. I cry and whine, and you listen. I don't know how you do it, but you never complain," she said as she gazed solemnly out the window.

"Grace you never asked for any of this and you're just trying to understand how to do this thing, this…task. You're doing all right, whose complaining?"

"I'm so glad and lucky to have you as friend, Delbert."

36

CHAPTER 13

Grace's father had built three small cabins out back, close to the barn, along the side of the apple orchard, for the itinerant workers that came to harvest the fruit every year, and Grace was cleaning them, readying them for occupation. She and her foreman had painted them white again and they were clean and inviting even though they were small.

The ladders were stacked and leaned against the back of the barn. The 12 and 16 foot ladders had stems and could stand alone, the 20 and 30 footers leaned against the tree. These were the ladders used for picking the cherries and apples off the trees.

The following week the Rodriguez family came to see Grace. It was a small family consisting of Julio, the father, Maria, the mother, Pablo, the oldest son, Juanita, the daughter and Lito, the youngest of the family. They had brought along a nephew, Julio's sister's son, who had been deserted because the sister could not take care of him. He was afflicted with Multiple Sclerosis. Julio, who did not need another mouth to feed, was forced to undertake the well being of Juan. Juan's disability was just another cross to struggle with, for the Rodriguez family.

"Señorita Grace, your heart is beeg or I would not come to you at thees time. Señor Hedges apples must be theened and he has given my family the job. But he has no place for us to stay. Your cabins are empty until the cherries become ready to harvest, yes. Each year you let us use one. Thees year, maybe early, no?"

She paused, "I think that would be all right."

"O, gracias, gracias, muchas gracias, Señorita Grace. Tank you, tank you," he crossed himself and ran toward the old car he was driving, but pulled up short and ran back to Grace.

"OK today?"

She nodded.

"Vaya con Dios, Señorita. Vaya con Dios!" Again he ran off to his car and again came back. "Señorita, por favor, come, come. Thees eze Juan Jose Ramon Feliciano, my, how you say, - - neeece."

Grace giggled amiably. "I think 'nephew' is the word you're looking for, Julio."

"Si, si, nephew, this is the word."

" Nice to meet you, Juan," she said through the open back window."

The thin young man squashed in the back seat along with Pablo, Juanita, Lito, and bags of clothes and food, turned his head to Grace spazmodically and whispered, "hola" with a mischievous grin. They all smiled shyly at Grace as Julio started the car and headed down the driveway toward the small white cabins.

Two days later Grace was opening the door to the cabin, adjacent to the one the Rodriguez family was using, to air it out when she heard what sounded like a body falling to the floor. She put her ear to the door and listened...heard nothing and reached for the knob again. Then she heard what sounded like something heavy being dragged across the wooden floor. She knocked on the door, "Hello? Is some one in there?" She knocked again, turned the knob slowly and pushed the door open. There was a surprised squinting Juan looking back at an equally surprised Grace.

"Are you all right?" she asked.

He said something in Spanish. She cocked her head and shrugged her shoulders to indicate she didn't understand. He said something else in Spanish then realized she didn't understand him.

He was wearing only a pair of white undershorts. She walked over to him and stood looking at his torso. There were few spots on his body that didn't have bruises.

"My God Juan, what happened?" she asked quietly as she approached him. *I've never seen anything like this*, she thought.

She closed her eyes and whispered, "God, this is not right. Grace knelt and put one hand on his shoulder. She closed her eyes and after a few seconds, opened them. He lay limp and quiet but she could hear him breathing.

He rolled onto his back and lay quietly. She slipped outside and looked back in through the window.

Juan looked around and when he didn't see Grace he called out to her. A look of confusion, fear passed over his face as he looked down at his legs.

The bruises were gone. He rolled over on his side and felt like he could stand, pushed himself up with his hands full on the floor and he was standing, tentatively. He took a few unsteady steps, then a few more. He turned around and around, then jumped in the air and started shouting in Spanish. He was laughing and crying at the same time. A feeling of wonder overtook him and he knelt, crossed himself and began to pray.

Grace silently said her own prayer of thanks and hurried away.

THE ENDOWMENT

CHAPTER 14

It was just a little before 7:30 and Grace had settled down to read *Of Mice and Men*. She was tired and wired at the same time. Sleep was what was needed and reading a book was sure to make her eyes heavy.

Suddenly, there was knock on the door and before she could get herself together, a more emphatic bang, then she heard him.

"Meese Grace, milagro, milgro," Julio shouted. "Venga, venga, come, Meese Grace. Milgro, milgro." As she opened the door, Julio grabbed her hand shouting "andele, andele" as he pulled her out and toward the cabin. He was yelling in Spanish and pulling her along as fast as he could.

They arrived at the cabin and Julio burst through the door. The family was on their knees, praying. Juan was in the center. Julio told him to stand. Julio said something else in Spanish and Juan took off his shirt. There were no bruises on his arms or chest. Julio, with tears rolling down his face, hugged Juan and danced. Grace realized that Juan did not recognize her as the person who had been there earlier.

"Un angel came to Juan while we were working today, and she shake him hard. She make him OK. mira! Look!"

Grace stepped toward Juan and opened her arms. He was hesitant. After all, he didn't really know this woman. But in the end he grinned shyly and stepped into her embrace. Then everyone hugged her for a moment.

"Thank you, Julio. This *is* a 'milagro'." She turned to the beaming family, I must go now, Buenos notches."

They all laughed and practically in unison said "Buenos notches."

She walked slowly home, happy with the results, and happy for the Rodriguez family. Juan would no longer have to endure all that self-imposed punishment. And he could take his place as another positive force in the little family, a means of more 'dinero', as Julio would say.

40

Two days later Jimmy Marr, Grace's foreman, and Grace were walking the orchard when Jimmy made a comment about the 'milagro.'

"Oh, you heard about the milagro," she said smiling.

"Julio was telling me in Spanish that some angel, a beautiful angel, had made Juan well."

"Your understanding of Spanish is certainly better then mine."

"I've always thought of angels as being women," he said.

"What about Lucifer and Gabrielle?" she mused, "So what's your point?"

"That's right, well, when he said an angel, I thought it might have been you."

"Why, Jimmy, what a sweet thought, me, an angel. Did he actually see this...angel?"

"My Spanish is pretty good, but sometimes I miss the most important word and I can't make any sense of it. I didn't get to see him before he had his milagro, but Julio said Juan was barely able to see, just outlines of people, and his hearing was bad too, because of his disease. Hard to believe, cause I talked to Juan and I swear, he doesn't look like there was ever anything wrong with him. Not that I don't believe him, Grace, but these people can be a little naive. You know what I mean?"

Grace nodded politely.

The next few days were quiet around her small farm and she got the opportunity to tell Delbert about Juan.

CHAPTER 15

It was Wednesday, June 6th, 1956. Delbert saw Grace and Jimmy walking into the apple orchard. He loped across his yard and caught them before they got too far into the rows of apple trees.

"Morning Grace, Jimmy."

"What's up Delbert?"

"June and I are going to Deaconess Hospital tomorrow evening, and just wanted to know if you wanted to come along?"

"What time?"

"Around six or six thirty.

"Can I think about it?"

"It's up to you."

The next day at 6:00 PM. Grace was standing by the Blair car.

"Is it still all right for me to tag along Delbert?"

"Glad to have you come with us, Honey," June said as she opened the door to the car.

The drive up Highway 28 was quiet and relaxing, with very little traffic.

"How are your Bing's coming along?" Grace asked.

"Delbert!" June poked him.

"I'm sorry, what did you say?"

"She wants to know how our Bing's are coming along?"

"I think in about another two weeks they should be ready to pick. How about yours?"

"About the same. Maybe three weeks?"

"Let's hope it doesn't rain and ruin them."

"I've been listening to the weather reports and no one's talking about rain."

"Let's hope it doesn't."

They crossed the bridge and started up the Steven Street hill.

"Who are we going to see at the hospital?" Grace asked.

"Her name is Delores Reiben, she's an old high school class mate. Guess she has to have a kidney removed," June responded.

"Is that a serious operation?"

"I guess it can be."

"Can you live with one kidney?"

"I think you can.

"Well, we're here," announced Delbert.

The three went up to the 4th floor and June walked off to see her friend. Grace and Delbert walked around the floor looking into the rooms.

"Hospitals can be depressing," Delbert whispered.

Grace nodded and stopped at a room with a single bed. She saw a patient, a young woman, lying on the bed. The bed appeared to have been made and the person on it had not moved a muscle since. Grace felt compelled to go into the room. Delbert stood outside the door of the room, looking inside. She walked quietly to the side of the bed and stood looking down at the pretty young face. After a few seconds she started to leave.

The young woman in the bed opened her eyes and looked up at the ceiling.

"Do I know you?"

Grace turned and came back to her bedside.

"No you don't," Grace said softly.

"You're not a nurse or a doctor are you?"

"That's right."

The young woman's eyes blinked quickly and then, tears were rolling down the sides of her face.

"I'm so sorry, I shouldn't have come in here,"

A nurse walked into the room, "Are you family?"

"I was just leaving," Grace said, as the brushed past the nurse and out the door. As she walked past Delbert, she dug in her purse for a handkerchief. They moved past the nurses' station and on to the waiting room.

"I don't know why I walked into her room," she said sadly as she wiped her eyes.

"Lately, things are hard to figure out," he said in a hushed voice.

"Sorry to keep you waiting," June said as she walked into the waiting room. "I'm hungry. Can we go get a Dusty Burger?"

"Ooooooohhhhh," Grace agreed.

CHAPTER 16

Thursday June 22, 1956. The cherry harvest season had arrived. There had been no rain, the sun had not burned the cherries and there were enough pickers. The equipment needed to haul the fruit from the orchard and the trucks to transfer the fruit to the warehouse had all held up. Wenoka Warehouse had given them a good price and everyone was happy.

Delbert, June and Grace were sitting outside on Grace's patio drinking a beer. It was a beautiful, warm evening. The apple harvest would begin at the end of September or in early October. The equipment was all ready, and all was right with the world.

"I've been thinking about taking my boat and going up to the lake and do some water skiing," Grace ventured.

"I'm not much of a water skier," June said finishing her beer and stood.

"Would you like another?"

"No thanks, hon. I've got a project to finish, so I'll be moseying along."

"How about you Delbert, would you like to go the lake and do a little water skiing?"

"I'm in."

"Well, everyone and their cousin will be up there this weekend. So how about Monday next?"

"Monday? Sure that'll be fine. Thanks for the beer. I've got to put the tractor in the barn. So I'd better go."

"Thanks for coming over, Delbert. Later."

CHAPTER 17

Delbert had been watching TV when June shook him gently and told him to go to bed.

"What time is it?"

"You've been snoring for the last fifteen minutes. I thought you were going to rattle the glasses off the shelves. It's a little after ten."

He picked up his shoes and headed off to his room. He hadn't been asleep very long when June came into the room and shook him again.

"June, I'm in bed," he said drowsily with a little irritation. "Delbert, maybe you'd better get up. Grace's dogs never bark, and now they're barking their heads. He jumped up and dressed quickly. "What time is it?"

"Almost midnight. You'll need a flashlight!"

He opened the door, funnel of light in hand and ran toward Grace's house. It was pitch dark. He tripped and almost fell and the flashlight fell from his hand s and went dark. Usually the light from the corral gave enough illumination, but tonight it was completely dark. His eyes were acclimating, but it was still too dark. He was almost to the front door when he stumbled against it.

The house was completely dark and the dogs were still growling and barking.

"Grace," he shouted and banged on the door. Nothing. "Grace," he yelled again.

He lowered his shoulder and slammed into the door with all his strength. It flew open and carried him into the front room. He couldn't see a thing. He stood motionless, trying get his bearings. Suddenly he was hit squarely in the face. His head banged solidly against the doorframe. It dazed him momentarily, but he was aware that someone ran by him and out the door. He struggled to his knees then reached out for the wall and stood, weak-kneed and wobbly.

"Grace," he yelled. The dogs were barking in a room, somewhere. He felt along the doorframe until he found the light switch.

THE ENDOWMENT

The room was intact. Everything seemed to be in place. He moved, as quickly as his dizziness would allow, to the door where the dogs were and opened it. Two very anxious dogs ran out and straight to Grace's room. Delbert followed, calling her name as he went.

The door was open. He stepped in, flipped the light on and walked over, to the bed, dreading what he was going to find.

Even so, he was not prepared for what he did find. Grace on her back, completely nude, except for a single strap from her nightgown wrapped around her shoulder. The rest of the garment was wadded under her. She appeared to be dead.

"Delbert! Delbert! June shouted, "Are you in there?"

"June, the back bedroom, hurry!"

She ran into the room carrying a big flashlight and stood at the foot of the bed. Delbert was immobile, as if he were nailed to the spot. She looked down at the bed, her hands covered her face and she gasped, "Is she dead?"

He was frozen. Anguish distorted his face. "I don't know! I don't know!"

She stepped around him and pulled the sheet over her. "Delbert go call an ambulance and the Sheriff...GO!"

The deputy Sheriff from the sub-station in Malaga arrived first. They exchanged names and he proceeded to the bedroom.

"You the folks that called it in?"

Both answered, "yes" simultaneously.

"This how you found her?"

"Yes," Del said sadly, "except June pulled the sheet over her."

He leaned over her, checked for a pulse, found a faint one, and checked to make sure she was breathing.

"She's alive! But somebody sure worked her over. If you don't sir, I'm going to ask you to go outside and wait for the ambulance, ma'am you can stay. Then, I'm going to seal off house for the investigators."

When Grace saw June she tried to sit up.

"Oh, June! Oh my God, June!" She tried to raise her arms, but the pain was too great. June rushed to her and hugged her gently.

46

"Did he rape me?" she sobbed.

"Oh, sweetie, you just take it easy now. I think the ambulance is here."

The two ambulance attendants rushed in, quickly checked her over and gently placed her on the gurney. June held her hand, and Grace sobbed as they rolled her out and to the ambulance.

"Can June go with me, please?"

June looked over at Delbert.

"I'll follow you up there," he said quietly, his pain plainly etched on his face.

THE ENDOWMENT

CHAPTER 18

The following day the Sheriff called the Wenatchee Police Department and talked to Chief Patrick Duffy about the possibility of borrowing Detective Kelli Finnigan.

"It's all right by me but I'll give you her extension."

"Finnegan."

"Good morning, detective, this is Sheriff Hobson. I just talked to your boss about borrowing you for an investigation and he said I should call you direct and ask you personally."

"Homicide?"

"It could have been, if not for a diligent neighbor. She was beaten and almost raped, at least that looks like what the perp had in mind."

"When?"

"Last night."

"Where is she?"

"Deaconess."

"Would I be working with someone?"

"I'm going to try to get you some help."

"When would I start?"

"When we hang up the phone."

"Your jurisdiction?"

"That's why I need to borrow you."

"Where does she live?"

"Palisades."

"Hmm, never been there."

"It's a blip in the road just the other side of Malaga."

"Well, if the Chief doesn't mind, I'll get started. You said Deaconess? I'll need her name."

"I guess that would help, it's J-E-N-N-I-N-G-S, Grace. Need anything else?"

"Not immediately."

"Thanks, I owe you one Detective."

Kelli checked her watch as she walked over to the Chief's office and verified she would assist on the case.

"I'm going to the hospital now."

48

"Fine Kelli, that's a good idea, this might be our perp, I'm not sure we have the right guy in jail."

"Did he give you some history on her?"

"No. He just told me that she was badly beaten and would have been raped, maybe killed, if not for her neighbor's alert action."

"OK Patrick, I'll try to be back around noon."

Kathleen Kelli Finnegan arrived at the hospital and was directed to room 418 where Doctor Tim Biner would be meeting with her. The door to the elevator opened on the fourth floor. She was met by a tall, bespectacled, sandy haired, man with a white doctor's coat and a stethoscope hanging from his front pocket.

"Detective Finnegan?"

"Dr. Biner?"

He led her to the visitor's room.

"She was beaten badly. There are facial lacerations and some bruising around the vagina, but no evidence of penetration. There are bruises on her shoulders, chest and arms. There was also trauma to her jaw from a hard slap or maybe a punch, a black eye and a fragile psyche at the moment. She has a large Nevus covering the left side of her face. If you've never seen her before you might wonder about it. She's had that from birth."

"Nevus?"

"Sorry, birthmark."

She nodded, "I sure would like to talk to her."

"Just for a few minutes."

They headed off to room 418.

"By the way, Detective this is a very special lady. In May she arrived here, dead, then miraculously, came to life. She wasn't meant to die then, and she won't now."

Kelli, acknowledged his words and then proceeded to 418. She quietly entered the two-bed ward and looked at the woman in the bed on the right side. She appeared to be sleeping. The bed was unruffled,

The other bed held the woman with the birthmark. She was staring directly at Kelli as she walked in.

49

THE ENDOWMENT

"Grace Jennings?" she asked in a hushed voice.

Grace stared at her suspiciously.

"I'm Detective Kelli Finnegan, from the Wenatchee Police Department.

At that moment a man and woman tentatively entered the room and came over to stand by the detective.

"Delbert! June!" Grace sobbed, "I'm so glad you're here."

June leaned over the bed and hugged Grace. Delbert stood back and eyed the woman suspiciously.

"Can I help you with anything?" as Delbert motioned for her to move into the hallway.

"I believe you can. You must be the neighbors?" I'm Detective Kelli Finnegan, can we talk. Maybe we can go to the visiting room. I need to be sitting down so I can read what I've written afterwards. I don't believe I got your last names, except for Delbert and June, "

"Our last name is Blair, June is my sister.

Now, this happened last night?"

"Yes."

"Tell me about it."

"Well, about midnight June woke me up to tell me the dogs were barking at Grace's house."

"How'd you know it was midnight?"

"I asked her when she woke me."

"All right, go ahead."

"I got dressed and took off for her house, it's about a hundred yards away, and when I got there I yelled out her name but she didn't answer."

"Were there any lights on in the house?"

"No, the place was completely dark. I yelled her name again. Again nothing. I knew something was wrong and the dogs were barking like mad. I stepped away from the door, put my shoulder to it and broke in. I stood for a few seconds and tried get my bearings. That's when somebody slugged me. I fell backward and hit my head on the doorframe. Then whoever hit me ran out the door. I found the light switch, went down the hall and let the dogs out. They ran straight to Grace's room. When I

50

got a glimpse of her I grabbed the dogs by their collars and pulled them outside. That's when June got there.

"Do you think it was only one person?"

"I believe so, and a pretty good sized one at that."

"How so?"

"Well, I've thrown some punches and taken a few and this one had some weight behind it. It was a pretty good punch."

"Tell me how you found Grace?"

"She was lying on the bed and she was---she was, well, she was naked. She looked like she had been in a fight. Honestly, I thought she was dead. June covered her and we waited for the ambulance and the Sheriff to show up. The deputy showed first and he checked her out. She was alive. If you ever catch this guy detective, I'd sure like to spend a few minutes with him...alone. Grace means a lot to me," he said, choking back the last couple of words.

Kelli could see that he was in pain, and was having difficulty, "Anything else?"

He shook his head.

"Thank you. You've been helpful and I know I'll need to talk more with you later. Would you mind asking your sister to come in?"

THE ENDOWMENT

CHAPTER 19

"Tell me what happened from when you first heard the
dogs barking, Miss Blair."

June told Finigan her side of the story.

"How far behind him were you?"

"Couldn't say for sure, maybe, a minute, a minute and a
half. "

"Did you see anyone run out of the house?"

"No."

"I understand. All right, thank you June."

They went back to room 418. Delbert and June told
Grace they would be back later and left Detective Finnegan
alone with Grace.

Kelli pulled a naugahyde chair up next to Grace's bed,
and as she sat she noted the wariness was gone from Grace's
eyes. Delbert had probably calmed her fears.

She pulled out her note pad and smiled at Grace, then
started slowly, asking questions about the ranch, the animals,
how long had she known the Blairs? After a while Grace took a
deep breath and looked Kelli in the eyes, "OK, I think I can tell
you about that awful night now."

Kelli asked if Grace had seen the rapist's face. She
hadn't. She asked her what she remembered about that night.

Grace took a deep breath, composed. She told the
detective she had put the dogs in their room and gone to bed
around midnight.

" You don't sleep in the same room with the dogs?" the
detective interjected. "No, I love my dogs but I prefer they sleep
in their own room." The detective nodded. "You went to bed at
midnight and---"

"No, it was eleven fifty five, she remembered thinking
she was getting to bed before midnight. About the only thing
that was unusual was that the light at the corral was out. She had
fixed that light after the big storm earlier in the year. She made a
mental note to check it out in the morning, she locked the front
and back doors."

52

Maybe, five minutes after she had crawled into bed a man put his hand over her mouth and whispered he would kill her if she screamed or refused to cooperate.

She had nodded and then punched at him where she thought his face would be. He in turn, punched her back and with a great deal of force and she temporarily lost consciousness. When she became aware again he was still hitting her. She screamed and fought him with all her might. He slapped her very hard and put his hands around her throat and squeezed. That was the last thing she remembered until she opened her eyes and there was a deputy checking her pulse.

"When I woke up this morning and realized where I was, I knew it had *not* been a nightmare. I felt dirty, so dirty - - all I wanted to do was take a bath," she choked out through her tears.

"I hope you catch the dirty son-of-bitch and hang him by his cojones," she spat between her clenched teeth.

Kelli gave her a minute to compose herself.

When she was under control again, she looked sheepishly at Kelly, "Forgive me detective, I think I'm better than that. I won't let this turn me into a bitter and vengeful woman, almost to herself, she promised I won't!!!"

"You're going to be OK. I can feel it," she comforted. "Grace, you did very well. I know it was hard, but we'll talk more later when you're feeling better. I'm going to do everything in my power to put this creep behind bars. Now as for you, you get well and I'll keep in touch."

Detective Finnegan found Delbert and June and asked if she could follow them home. She had heard about the small town of Palisades, but had never been there. She wanted to walk through Grace's house, which was hopefully still draped with yellow crime scene tape, and uncontaminated. They went to Grace's room to say their good-byes, and left the hospital.

CHAPTER 20

Kelli Finnegan drove down the road from the Blair's home to Grace Jenning's driveway. The single story home was well maintained and spacious, surrounded by a variety of flowers and bushes. There was a large barn and a corral in back of the house.

This woman loved flowers and animals and obviously knew a lot about orchards, Kelli thought, as she looked out at the apple and cherry orchards. She heard a dog bark, turned around to find a beautiful white and tan Collie and a handsome Rottweiler staring at her.

"So you're the two birds that started all the commotion that brought the good neighbors to your mistress's rescue?"

They seemed harmless enough, she thought as she held out her hand. They sniffed it, licked it and walked to the porch. Strange these dogs knew when to bark. She had read or heard somewhere that some animals have gone for help when their master is incapacitated or in danger. Some are even killed defending the 'leader of their pack'.

She could see the bolt and lock on the door were askew and the doorframe shattered from Delbert's aggressive entry. Pushing the door open, she stepped into a pristine living room and walked down the hall to the bedroom. She ducked under the yellow tape and into the room. Standing at the foot of the bed, she scanned the room for any incongruities.

"Detective Finnegan, are you in there?"

" Is that you Tracy? I'm in the back bedroom."

Tracy. leaned under the tape, pulling a handcart stacked with boxes, bags and tags.

"You been here long?"

"Just got here. Boy, you come prepared. Looks like you've got enough stuff to bag the whole room."

"Well, figured we'd have to take the bed stuff cause you said she'd been attacked in bed. Need some rubber gloves?"

"Thanks."

54

Kelli walked over to the bedroom window and observed the curtains moving slightly with the gentle breeze. She pulled the curtains aside and saw the lower window had been pushed all the way up.

"I think I have some semen on the sheet and some pubic hair. There's blood all over. If we're lucky some of it may be his."

Tracy took pictures of the bed, the floor, the window and the room in general. Next came the fingerprint dust.

Outside she dusted the window and got a picture of a partial large shoe print. Although it was not a complete clear print it did have some detail, maybe enough to match, if they found the shoe.

Detective Finnegan came around the corner of the house and stopped a few feet from the open window.

"Tracy, that was the only window that was open. What do you think? Is this our point of entry?"

"Well, I checked the rest of the house and it appeared to be clean. If I had to guess, I'd say our man probably came through this window and then waited for the lady to come to bed, watched her till she fell asleep, then attacked her. Looks like he knows what he's doing. Maybe done it before."

"You should have been a policewoman, Tracy."

"Thank you, I consider that a complement. How do you see it?"

"Same as you, the only question I have is where did this guy park?"

"Well, I did notice there's a clump of poplar trees surrounded by some Mayten bushes that could hide a car, just after you leave highway 28,"

"Mayten bushes?"

"Yes, I only noticed them because they're pretty rare around here and it was unusual to see them out there, in the wild – so to speak. They're indigenous to Chile, but have gained some popularity in Southern California and Florida. I tried to raise one, but it never worked out. "Tracy Forbush, you're fantastic. I'll check it out. How long a walk would that be?"

"Probably 'bout three quarters of a mile, maybe less."

THE ENDOWMENT

"Would you mind going out there with me? With any luck we may get some shoe prints or tire tread."

"Let's do it!"

CHAPTER 21

Eighteen days had passed since that night and Grace had been staying with the Blairs. Delbert had fixed the door and June had completely changed Grace's bedroom. The two dogs would now be sharing her old room and she would be using the guest room, which was the nicer bedroom.

Dr. Angelina Lansing, a psychiatrist whose practice was based in Wenatchee, had been brought in by the Rape Unit Group to work with Grace. She had seen her Monday, Wednesday and Friday for two weeks. Grace had benefited from the counseling. Though reticent to move back home, she swallowed her fears and moved back and into her new bedroom. Delbert had volunteered to sleep in the dog's old room for as long as she wanted while she adjusted.

"You really are my special guy."

Delbert wanted to tell Grace he would stay as a permanent guest if she so desired. He would do anything to keep her safe, not that it would be a hardship for him to move in for a while. He treasured every minute in her presence, he loved her. Del hadn't admitted it, even to himself. Just let someone try to come into this house without Grace's approval.

The phone rang.

"Would you mind answering that for me, Delbert?"

"Hello," he said quietly.

"Is this the Grace Jennings residence?"

"May I ask who's calling?"

"Joan Demmek."

He put his hand over the mouthpiece. "It's Joan Demmek."

"I'll talk to her."

Delbert walked to the kitchen. Grace talked for a few minutes and then came into where Delbert was standing.

"She's been worried about me. Said she tried to call and was unable to reach me. So she's coming to see me tomorrow."

"Are you ready to do God's work?"

"Honestly, I don't know."

THE ENDOWMENT

"Well, this Joan lady is pretty convincing."

"She does have a way about her," she said smiling.

"You don't suppose she and the guy upstairs are in cahoots - - maybe ganging up on you?"

"Maybe. But I've got a guardian angel."

Delbert flushed and stammered. Grace chuckled at his discomfort, then laughed. Del couldn't help himself and soon they were both laughing.

CHAPTER 22

Joan Demmek arrived at noon and greeted Grace like a long lost friend.

Grace led her into the kitchen, where Delbert was reading the paper. He stood when they entered, greeted Joan, and made a move to leave.

"Hi Mr. Blair, good to see you. How's June?" She removed her sweater and placed it on the back of a chair. I tried to call you. B-L-A-I-R, right? They said there were no Blairs in the phone book."

"We're not listed, by preference, and June is fine."

"I'm sorry Mr. Blair. Here I am spouting off like a machine gun. I guess it's the long ride that makes me chatter like an unhappy blue jay. I was really worried about Grace to begin with, and then when I couldn't reach her, I didn't know anyone else to call. So what's the story and I'll shut up and listen."

"Delbert, would you mind staying?" Grace asked softly. "Sit down Joan, would you like a cup of coffee?"

Grace poured out the sordid story, telling it like it had happened to someone else. Joan listened intently. Tears rolled down her face and she forgot the coffee and walnut filled oatmeal cookies Grace had put in front of her. Delbert sat quietly.

"Oh my God, Grace how could this happen? Why would,why would He make you special and then allow such a terrible thing to happen to you?"

She reached into her purse, pulled out a handkerchief, rushed over to Grace and hugged her compassionately. They stood, entwined, crying and patting each other. Delbert was feeling uncomfortable and walked over to the kitchen window and looked out at the corral.

"He can't be mad at you. Of course not! God doesn't do those things. He made you special, don't you see?"

Grace shook her head sadly and moved back to the table. Joan sat down across from her, took her hand and looked imploringly into her eyes.

THE ENDOWMENT

"I don't know why God would allow such a thing Grace, but I know he'll see you through it," she sniffed.

They sat, Joan trying to see into Grace's soul. Grace was lost in her own confused thoughts.

"Grace you can't stop using something God has given you to help people. You said it yourself, He could have picked someone else, but he didn't. He chose you. Surely you believe that, don't you?"

"I don't know, Joan. Right now I don't know what to think. I've been robbed of my dignity, my self-assurance, my lust for life, and my sense of worth. I feel like my soul has been tainted with doubt. Dr. Lansing told me I would feel some depression, and I have. Some times I cry for no reason and my appetite has all but left me. You were kind enough not to mention my weight loss. I've had thoughts about whether I should even go on living. All these things were foreign to me less than three weeks ago." She pulled out another tissue and blotted her eyes.

"Oh Grace, I am so sorry. It's impossible to feel what you must be going through." Joan's voice was swallowed by the tears.

"I think I need a little more time before I'm ready to face the world again." Grace stood, walked over to Joan and put her arm around her shoulder. "I consider you a good friend and hope you understand I just need some more time to myself."

"I do, I do." She stood, turned, hugged Grace, and in between sobs, asked if there was anything she could do for her. She went over to Delbert and hugged him, said her good-byes and hurried out.

60

CHAPTER 23

"I'm going for a walk Delbert. I'll be back in a little while.

She walked slowly up the road until she came to the fork that led to the Blairs, then by-passed it for a path that hugged the hills along to the box canyon. Her thoughts went back to Joan and their short discussion. Just talking about it had magnified the effect this whole wretched nightmare had imposed on her life. She no longer felt the breeze in her face, didn't smell the sweet fragrance of alfalfa or the redolence of cherry blossoms, the cooing of the doves, or the celebrating blackbirds in the nearby fields. She missed watching the humming birds on her Cape Cod Honey Suckle, the tufts of dandelions on the roadside, the screeching of the Red Tailed Hawk high in the air. All these she had been missing, and more.

The nights were worse. It was like a giant black cloud had claimed the days and kept out the sun. Bits and pieces of memory, longing to be forgotten, but etched indelibly in the recesses of her brain were pushed to the forefront, not to be ignored by turning from side to side or squeezing her eyes closed. The nights seemed endless, only the dawn a brought a welcome degree of respite.

She had unconsciously turned around at some point and was on the road home. When she arrived she found Delbert sitting at the kitchen table reading, "1984."

"It seems so far away, doesn't it?" she said pointing to the book.

"You all right?"

"Well, not completely, but I think I do feel better," she smiled sadly.

CHAPTER 24

Grace was up early today, earlier than most days even though she was able to sleep better now. She was thinking of her mother and some of the things she used say to her. Her mother lived by simple rules. 'Work hard, eat well and you sleep sound.' Grace had wondered on occasion when she was growing up why she didn't have any brothers or sisters. Her mother had told her once it was because she couldn't. She never explained why and it was never brought up again. Her mother loved her and never forgot to tell her. It was always simply stated but it was precise. She believed her mother. Sometimes she felt lonely for her mother and her father. She was experiencing some of that loneliness now. How many times had she walked with her quiet mother through their orchard? Grace thought it was the reason she was quiet. Her father had been a man of few words too. Though when either spoke it was exactly what they had to say.

She stopped by the edge of the orchard and looked up at the sky. It was dark blue with millions of diamonds winking down at her. She felt special with the morning chill nipping her body and making her glad to be alive. She heard the hoot of a barn owl on the fence that separated the field from the apple trees.

A large Jackrabbit stopped on the road, twenty yards away and stared at her, then scampered into the grass and sagebrush and disappeared. A dove cooed for her mate from an apple tree. As she continued her walk she saw three Does and a little one feeding on dandelion and wild alfalfa between the road and the fence. When she stepped on a twig, they stopped and looked her way, then strolled off. She had walked about three hundred yards and was now at the back of her acreage. She looked up at the sky again and as if by magic the stars had been erased. She could see clear across the way to the jutting hills that composed the box canyon.

"Trouble sleeping?" Delbert asked trying not to frighten her.

"Morning Delbert. No, I'm sleeping much better."

"You were up early, even for you.

"I'm sure glad you keep an eye on me, cause sometimes I think I'm all alone, then, like magic, there you are. I hope you'll always be around."

He didn't know how to respond to her, his feelings were too deep and he was afraid he would scare her away. He managed to choke out, "We'd better stop here. There's a Gopher snake on the road up there."

"Yuk, I can't stand snakes. I know that Gopher snakes are non-venomous but I'm still afraid of them. You would think after all the years I've lived here and all the ones I've seen I'd get over them. I guess I'm just a big scaredy cat," she said and nuzzled up to Delbert. She looked up at him and he blushed.

"I've embarrassed you. I'm just afraid of snakes."

"I suppose we're all afraid of something."

"What are you afraid of, Delbert?"

"I'm not sure, I know I have fears and they're real, but right now I can't think of my fears. I assure you I have real fears.

Today, as they walked along the road, each lost in their own thoughts, Del felt awkward. Sometimes when he was around Grace he would get tongue-tied and couldn't think straight. When she touched him affectionately it threw him off completely. He was aware that he blushed and that she noticed him blushing. They rounded a corner in the road and her two dogs came loping up to them, tails wagging.

"It's strange that your dogs don't bark unnecessarily, only when it counts. You hardly notice they're around. They remind me of cats."

"I've had them since they were pups and they have always been quiet. I didn't train them not to bark, they just don't bark. But boy, did they bring you to my rescue in the nick of time. Come in and have a cup of coffee with me, I think I've still got a couple of maple bars and some doughnuts in the refrigerator." She made some Folgers coffee and pulled out two large maple bars.

"Grace I know it's none of my business and I probably shouldn't be putting my two cents in but---well, you've saved

THE ENDOWMENT

those people already and you've managed to be discreet about it, but what's going to happen when the cat gets out of the bag."

"Believe me Delbert, that very thought has troubled me more than anything else. Honestly, I don't know. You're right, we've been lucky so far." She looked deep into her coffee cup and thought about the situation.

"God's kind of put you in the limelight with this gift."

"Honestly, I felt better about God when He wasn't so--- so personal. Delbert he's put you in the thick of it too, though. I feel like you're right here beside me, and I don't feel alone. I hope you're going to stay at my side always. I really believe I couldn't do this without you. I know God is at my side, at least, I choose to believe He is right here, even as we speak, but after what happened to me, I get scared and I wonder…good grief, what am I saying? I'm blithering like a schoolgirl." She felt stressed and rushed to the bathroom. After a while she came back to the kitchen table, her eyes and nose touched with red, and sat down. "God sure picked a big crybaby. For the life of me, I'll never know why. What criteria did He use to pluck me out of all the people in this world? Maybe, if I keep whining, he'll give up on me." Sobs wracked her again, but she managed to stammer, "Delbert if you want to leave I'll understand, I'm not very pleasant company right now."

Delbert looked at Grace and felt overwhelmingly close to her and wondered where all this was leading. What was going to happen to Grace? There must be a point where this will all end. Grace hadn't asked for any of this and now it was weighing heavily on her. There was no recourse, que sera, sera. Yes, he would stay at her side as long as she wanted him around. He did wonder, would this special endowment eventually disappear as quickly as it had come or would she have to die to be free of its power?

"Grace I'm sorry I brought the subject up," he took her hand, "and I'm not going anywhere. I'll always be here for you."

64

CHAPTER 25

"Hi, is this Grace Jennings?"

"Yes, it is."

"This is Katherine Penny. I'm not sure you'll remember me."

"The name doesn't ring a bell. Can you tell me where we met?"

"We were in the hospital at the same time." There was a pause.

"Oh yes, I remember you now, Katherine. How did you get my number?"

"My mother looked it up from your hospital stay, I hope you don't mind."

"I'm glad you did. How are you doing, Katherine?"

"I'm doing as well as I'm able, under the circumstances, but I didn't call to talk about me, I wanted to know how you were doing."

"I'm doing well, honestly. I'm touched that you would call to check on me. That's a very generous thought. I've been thinking about you and would like to come and see you sometime."

'That would be great. You sound good, Grace. Somehow I thought you might sound a little different."

"If you had called a couple of weeks ago, you would have been talking to a different person. What happened to me was bad, but it could have been worse."

"I'm happy for you, Grace."

"Some times it's hard to understand God's way."

"I'm not talking to God right now, not feeling very Christian like."

There was a pause.

"Give me a day that I can come and see you Katherine, and I'll be there."

She could hear her conferring with her mother.

"Sorry to keep you waiting Grace, would tomorrow be all right?"

THE ENDOWMENT

"Tomorrow's fine. What's a good time?"

"Whatever suits you, I'm not going anywhere."

"I have a friend who goes with me almost every where I go. Would you have any objections if he came with me?"

"Not at all, it's nice to have friends like that, please bring him along."

"We're early risers, so would 9:00 A.M. be too early for you?"

Katherine gave her the address and directions. "I'll be waiting for you."

CHAPTER 26

The next morning as Grace and Delbert were crossing the bridge into Wenatchee they were talking again about Grace's endowment.

Delbert thought again of the power, and wondered if it would disappear. He ratcheted up his courage and decided to address his concerns. "I know I've brought this up before and maybe I shouldn't voice it now, but where is all this going. Is there an end to all this someday?"

She paused to think of the question. "That's occurred to me too, but I put it out of my mind, because it still doesn't seem real to me. If I think about it too much, I feel like I'm going crazy. Honestly, Delbert, I can't think about it. There are times that I think I'm dreaming and I'm going to wake up and it will all have been some strange dream; that I'm just a regular person, my old self. See I'm starting to get rattled. I get confused, so I try not to think too far ahead.

"It's just as confusing to me and June. We've tried to make sense of all that has happened to you and just don't have any answers."

"How far up Washington Street do we go before we hit Pershing?"

"According to the map it should be about two more blocks and to the right."

"Hi, my name is Grace Jennings and this is Delbert Blair. We're here to see Katherine Penny."

"She's expecting you. I'm her mother, Sandra. Thank you for coming to see her, she needs the company. I'll get another chair.'"

Katherine was sitting up in a wheel chair, with her arms on the armrests. She welcomed them with an inviting smile.

Beside the wheel chair was a hospital bed. The room had the touch of young woman who had been very active at school. Hanging on the wall were Wenatchee High School purple and

THE ENDOWMENT

gold pom poms and banners among pictures of classmates. A tennis racquet leaned against the wall, a softball sat on top of the dresser next to a set of bongo drums. Her cheerleading outfit could be seen hanging in the closet.

She watched as Grace and Delbert surveyed the room and her eyes welled. Grace went over to her and hugged and kissed her on the cheek. Delbert pulled his chair closer to the door and sat. Grace pulled out some tissues and wiped away Katherine's tears.

"Thank you for coming to see me, I didn't call you for that reason. I really wanted to find out how you were doing." Her eyes shifted over to Delbert.

"Katherine, this is Delbert Blair, my neighbor and wonderful friend."

"Hi Delbert."

"Nice to meet you Katherine."

"He found me just in time that terrible night."

"Oh, he was there?"

"Well, not exactly. He came running after the dogs started barking. Would you like to hear the story of what happened? I believe I can talk about it now without falling apart."

"Only, if you want to and it won't upset you."

Grace told the story again.

"You're a very brave woman, Grace," she choked through tears.

Grace looked down at Katherine and felt a rush of compassion. Delbert moved over to the window and looked out at the street to keep from becoming depressed.

After a few minutes, when the two had their composure back, Grace spoke.

"Katherine, would you mind if we closed the door for a few minutes?"

"I wouldn't mind, Grace, but my mother might get concerned. May I ask why?"

"I have a special talent and I would like to try it on you, with your permission, of course."

"Mother, I'm going to close the door for a few minutes, so don't get crazy. OK?" she yelled.

68

Sandra Penny came into the room and looked at Katherine without saying a word.

"Mother it's personal. Just a little privacy and only for a few minutes please."

Her mother looked over at Delbert.

"He has to stay," Katherine stated flatly.

"You're going to be all right?" Sandra asked tentatively.

"She'll be fine with us Mrs. Penny. I assure you we wouldn't harm your daughter."

She turned and left the room, pulling the door closed behind her.

"I'm going to put your hands together and then I'm going to clasp them in mine. Delbert is going to be standing on the other side of you because you may slide out of your wheel chair."

"My mother and brother have strapped me to the chair so I won't slide out."

"We're going to loosen the cloth belts around you so you'll have some room to move. OK?"

"Move? Well, if you think it's important I guess it's all right. I'm in your hands now Grace."

"I'm going to ask you to close your eyes and not to open them until I tell you."

"OK," and closed her eyes tightly.

Grace sandwiched both of Katherine's hand in hers and looked up. Grace stiffened, and then shuddered and jerked and then dumped her into Delbert's waiting arms.

He caught her and toppled backward. The wheelchair fell over sideways.

Grace had been thrown backward flat on the floor. The raucaus brought Sandra Penny bursting into Katherine's room. She was frozen in the doorway staring at the trio.

"What happened? What's going on here?" she screamed and ran to her daughter's side.

Delbert, who was gently holding Katherine, spoke in a calm voice, "Please, Mrs. Penny. I know it looks bad, but I assure you it's not. Katherine is fine, as you'll see in another minute or so. Could you please check to see how Grace is?"

THE ENDOWMENT

Sandra Penny turned and looked down at Grace's contorted face. Grace's eyes fluttered open and she stood precariously.

"Is she all right?" Grace whispered.

"Oh my God. My knee hurts, I must have hit it on the bed," Katherine said as she looked into Delbert's face.

"Katherine, say that again," Sandy declared.

Grace peered, still dopey, at the two on the floor.

"Mother, my hand is on my knee…and I can feel it," she bawled hysterically. "I can feel my knee, I can feel my knee. Oh, I'm sorry Delbert. I'm sure you don't like me yelling in your face, but I can feel my knee. " Mom, I believe I can stand if I can get out of this chair. I'm all tangled up in it. Can you help me?" Without thinking she moved her body to one side.

"I just moved! Mother, did you see?"

Her mother, equally shaken, was trying to remove the last of the soft belts that were securing Katherine to the wheelchair as fast as she could.

Delbert was lying on his back, with one leg under the wheel chair. When the belts had finally been removed, Katherine looked up and spoke.

"Mother I'm free of the belts, would you help me see if I can stand?"

Sandra Penny stood and helped Grace stand and then leaned over the side of the wheel chair. She put her arms under Katherine's and lifted her to her feet. Delbert slid his foot out from under the chair and stood up. Katherine stood waveringly, awe struck, looking at her mother, not believing what she was doing.

"I can feel the strength coming back in my body, Mother."

She looked over at Grace and walked shakily to her, put her arms around her and sobbed, "thank you, thank you, thank you." She held her for a long minute and just sobbed. Her mother joined the hug, and Delbert just stood by nodding his head in affirmation of the whole thing.

70

CHAPTER 27

Nine days later, Bob Dempsey had gotten a tip from a friend who knew a friend that knew someone that had seen a miracle unfold. The story was just too good to pass up. This was the real thing, the contemporary Notre-Dame de Lourdes in the Department of Hautes Pyrenees, France and the poor fourteen-year old Bernadette Soubiroux, 1858.

Grace B. Jennings was forty four years old, 1956. Could there be some spiritual connection?"

His boss at the Seattle Times had given him his blessed permission to pursue the story in the small town of Palisades, Washington.

He had arrived in Wenatchee and drove into a gas station to get directions to Deaconess Hospital.

After haggling with the information desk at the hospital about information that could and could not be given out to just anyone, he was referred to Dr. Tim Biner.

"Hi, Mr. Dempsey. I'm Dr. Biner, and I understand you're looking for information on Grace Jennings? And you work for the Seattle Times. What makes you think she was in this hospital?"

"I know she was admitted DOA and that she came back to life."

"Who gave you this information?"

"I'm not at liberty to tell you that."

They stood staring at each other in a Mexican stand off.

"Look Dr. Biner, you must have been the doctor who pronounced her DOA. I think I can understand your wanting to protect her, but this story needs to be told. The public would love to read a story about a real live miracle in the year of 1956. I'm not going to write a bunch of garbage or negative innuendoes about this woman, or what happened to her. I just want to write a good story about a good person doing good things for other people. We *do* write good stories occasionally." He handed the doctor a business card.

" So you really are with the Seattle Times."

Bob nodded.

THE ENDOWMENT

"Would it be possible to talk to the doctor who pronounced her dead?"

"Well, that would be me."

Dr. Biner led him to his office and told him the story. Dempsey was writing it all down. When Dr. Biner finished, Bob asked about the miracles.

"What miracles, other than the miracle of Grace coming back to life?" He looked at Bob intently. "You've heard something about her that we don't know here?"

Bob pulled a small notebook out of his briefcase, licked his thumb and started leafing through it until he found what he was looking for.

"Did you recently have a young woman, Katherine Penney in this hospital who was a quadriplegic?"

He nodded. "Where did you get this information?"

"Legally, Dr. Biner, I assure you. I have not broken any laws."

"What kind of information do you have concerning Miss Penny?"

"Well, it's wonderful information and it will please you, but I don't like that it's me telling you're unaware of this information." He looked directly at Dr. Biner. "My source tells me she's back to playing sports and will be cheer leading again. She's ambulatory."

"That's impossible. I saw her lab results myself and there is no way she could be walking, much less participating in any sports."

"I've got a map and I'm going up there now, would you like to come along?"

"You just try and stop me. Let me tell the staff I'm leaving the hospital. I'll be right back."

Dr. Biner directed Bob Dempsey to the Penny home.

Katherine Penny opened the door and stood there, speechless, looking at them, completely surprised.

"Dr. Biner, what a surprise. Please come in," she said with a very big smile.

He walked in entirely flabbergasted, and could do nothing more than stare at Katherine, speechless.

72

"Dr. Biner, how nice to see you," Sandra Penny said as she came into the front room. "Who's your friend?"

"Oh, oh, I'm sorry, this is Bob Dempsey.

"How did this happen, I don't understand, I saw your X-rays and labs, and…here you are. I mean I'm thrilled for you, but how can this be?"

They all looked at each other, Katherine smiling happily, Mrs. Penny blissfully spirited. Dr. Biner and Bob Dempsey were given the details of the whole experience by Katherine and Sandra Penny; they answered all of their questions as completely as they were able.

When they arrived back at the hospital, Dr. Biner opened the car door, then turned back and told him earnestly, "Mr. Dempsey, if you say anything *bad* about Grace Jennings, I will change my vocation from doctor to vigilante and hunt you down, do you understand?"

"Perfectly."

CHAPTER 28

The next day as Bob Dempsey was driving down Highway 28 he was noticing and appreciating the fruit trees that lined the highway. *Pretty country*, he thought. *Wonder what the winters are like around here?* Never realized the Columbia River ran so far up the middle of the state. Let's see now? That must be Rock Island Dam and Palisades is around three miles up 28, and to the left. He kept checking his odometer for the mileage and he was sure the next left was the road he would take to Palisades. *There it is*, he thought; *up this road for about two miles and then left again. I guess this is what they mean by the boondocks. This is desolate. Aha, there's the road and it goes right through that orchard. It sure stands out, up here, where there is nothing else. Well,* he thought *as he drove up to where there were two houses, one on the left and one to the right, I'll try the one on the left first.*

He stepped up on the porch and the door opened.

"Could I help you?"

"You certainly can. I'm looking for Grace Jennings."

She eyed him suspiciously, making him feel like an interloper.

"What do you want with her?" she asked contentiously.

"Are you Grace?"

"Who wants to know?" Delbert asked as he came to the door.

"Hello there, my name is Bob Dempsey and I was looking for Grace Jennings." He extended his card to the man.

"You with the Seattle Times?"

"Yes sir I am, and I've come along way to talk to Miss Jennings. If this isn't her house, that must be her house over there."

"What would the Times want with Grace?"

"We'd like to write a story about her. We think it would be a good human-interest story, nothing negative. I understand she has a very special talent, and well, with all the bad stories

JOSEPH F. MONTOYA

that get printed nowadays, we thought an upbeat story like Grace's would pick up the spirits of all the Times readers."

"What if she doesn't want to be written about?"

"I think I can appreciate those feelings. No offence sir, but I like to hear those words from Miss Jennings."

"I'm sorry, my name is Delbert Blair and this is my sister, June."

"Hello, it's nice to meet you, and I guess I'll drive down the road," he said and turned to leave, then hesitated and turned back. "She's very lucky to have good neighbors like you folks." Then he turned and strolled to his car.

"Hold on, Mr. Dempsey, if you don't mind the short walk I'll go with you."

"Thank you, Mr. Blair, I appreciate it."

They started toward Grace's house and Bob asked, "How long have you known Miss Jennings?"

"The properties we have now, belonged to our parents before they passed on."

"So you've known each other all your lives?" Bob ventured.

Delbert nodded, "Yes we have, but only as neighbors. We've always respected each other's privacy. But make no mistake, there's nothing I wouldn't do to protect Grace."

They arrived at the front door just as Grace opened it and stood in the doorway.

"I saw you coming down the road," she said and invited them in, eyeing the stranger cautiously. "Let's go into the kitchen."

Delbert and the man sat. Grace poured three cups of coffee and joined them at the table. Bob Dempsey thought Delbert would introduce him to Grace but he said nothing.

"Miss Jennings, my name is Bob Dempsey, and I've driven over from Seattle to see about writing a story about you."

"Why in heaven's name would you want to do a story about me?"

"Because it appears you have a talent, that quite frankly, has been let out of the bag. If it's true, it's a big story. I obtained this information from a reliable source, but he got it from an anonymous source that got it from another anonymous source

75

and that's the reason I'm here now. I was at the Penny residence yesterday with Dr. Biner and saw, what according to Dr. Biner, was a modern miracle."

Grace looked sadly at Dempsey and then over to Delbert.

"I suppose it was only a matter of time before someone would breach our trust. I'm surprised, and at the same time, I've been expecting it to happen. Delbert and I have tiptoed around the subject a few times, and hoped that, maybe, it wouldn't happen. Whom do you work for?"

"I'm with the Seattle Times newspaper." He observed Grace, looking to see why the Almighty would pick someone like her to perform the extraordinary. She seemed ordinary enough; there was a huge birthmark on her face, if removed, would allow her beautiful face to shine. She had a model's figure, slender, slightly muscular and a little taller than average, however, Grace did look like a farm girl, possibly due from the setting and dress attire.

"This isn't meant to sound disrespectful, Miss Jennings, but why do you think you were picked out of all the people in this world?"

"Look at me, Mr. Dempsey, what do you see about me that seems unique? I have done nothing to deserve it and, not to sound irreverent, I'm having difficulty trying to understand where this path is taking me, as well as my friends, Delbert and June. I've been battling this question since it happened. You have no idea what this thing is doing to my mind. One day I'm walking the perimeter of my small orchard and then I wake up in the hospital, supposedly killed by bolt of lightning and you seem to know the rest."

Dempsey was stumped. This was a real person, and so ordinary that he could understand her plight; an ordinary person in an extraordinary position.

"Have there been others, either before or since Miss Penny?"

She looked over at Delbert. He looked at the ceiling and took a drink of his coffee.

"Yes, counting the dove, there were three others."

76

"Well, I've not heard anything about those, so none of those were leaked. Would you have any objection on elaborating on them?"

She nodded and gave him as much detail as she could remember.

"Have you heard from any of these people that you've helped?"

"No, not really."

"What about Joan Demmek, up in Omak?" Delbert interjected.

"That's right. I have heard from Joan and she referred me to one of the families."

"Bob nodded.

"So, Joan Demmek came to see you because of her curiosity about the bolt of lightning that killed you. Right? Thinking you might have some kind of healing power because her mother's father told her a story about a peasant girl. And this girl had a situation that was reminiscent to yours?"

She nodded. "Then you saw a migrant worker, who you think had Multiple Sclerosis and you cured him, without anyone ever knowing it was you.

"Then, of course, there was Katherine Penny, who I was privileged to meet. You've been a busy woman, Grace."

The conversation stopped and she got the coffee pot and poured them some more coffee. Dempsey was busy writing this all down in his notepad.

"Someone broke into my house, and I was attacked after the first two cures, and nearly killed. I would have been except for my friend, Delbert."

Bob stopped writing and looked at Grace as if she had just thrown ice water in his face.

"You were attacked!" he said as he sat forward, stunned, but eager to hear the details.

"You've been smiled on by God, and then you're attacked in your own home. Not that life always makes sense, but this borders on ludicrous."

Delbert and Grace said nothing, just watched Bob's face as he tried to absorb the incredible information.

THE ENDOWMENT

Grace felt Bob's empathy for her. It was gratifying to think someone who saw a lot of life, and was identifying with her emotions.

Bob took a breath, leaned forward and began writing again. He stopped, gazed into Grace's eyes and said, "I hope you're going to let me write about you Grace."

She looked over at Delbert and waited for some sign from him, some indication of his feelings. After a few moments he pursed his lips and nodded ever so slightly. Bob, who had followed Grace's gaze, saw the small sign and smiled.

"Before I send anything I've written to my editor, I will have you proof read it for your approval. OK?"

"That sounds fair to me. Delbert?"

He nodded.

"One last thing to do here, and it's my problem. You do not exactly live in the city limits of the nearest town, which I guess is Wenatchee, and this place is probably considered out of the way, so I need to find a place to stay for awhile. Someplace close to you and Delbert. Any suggestions?"

"Well, June and I have a small cabin in the back of our house, by the barn that you could use," he offered, "but you'll have to give me a few days to clean it up. Hasn't been used for a few years."

"That's all right Delbert, he can stay in one of my cabins. They're all available now and there is no reason why he can't use one of them, but thank you."

"That's mighty generous of you, Grace, but I'm prepared to pay for the use of it. My budget allows for room and board. I just need to keep all my receipts.

"That won't be necessary. I allow the workers that come to harvest the fruit to use the cabins without cost, so there's no reason to charge you."

For the next hour and a half hour Del and Bob, discussed what kind of people they would seek to heal and where to search for them, other than the hospital. Bob wanted to know if the individual had to be in a mortal stage or merely handicapped in some capacity, mentally, blind, confined to a bed or a wheel chair, old, young. Would she travel, and if so, how far?

78

"We need to set up parameters for what we will do and how far we will travel to do this thing." Bob proclaimed

Grace had listened patiently, waiting for the men to come to the conclusion that they didn't need rules. When it appeared they might not arrive there on their own, she inserted, "Bob I don't think I want this to be some kind of business."

"Grace so far you've been discreet and it has worked for you but when the word spreads that you're a healer, watch the flood gates open. You'll have every Tom, Dick and Harry, at your door. Every lame, blind, mute, handicapped person will be seeking you out, believe me."

"Bob, I believe that God will lead those I'm supposed to help to me, or me to them. I don't think we can try to apply human operational parameters, or rules, to my activities. I go where He tells me to go."

"You're right. There is no printed manual for curing the sick and healing the handicapped through the power of God."

The issue was resolved. No rules!

He would return to Seattle to pick up his wardrobe for an indefinite stay in the Wenatchee area. He wished to be called if something came up while he was in Seattle and he would rush back. Today was Friday and he planned to return by the following Tuesday or Wednesday.

CHAPTER 29

The following Tuesday, Grace had fixed breakfast for Delbert and they were chatting over eggs and toast when there was an urgent knock on the door. Three men in dark hoods with pistols in their hands rushed into the front room, grabbed him and forced him into the kitchen. Grace was standing with the coffee pot in her hand, fright and confusion in her eyes.

"Are you Grace Jennings?" one of the men growled.

She put the coffee pot down, and tried to answer, fear constricted her throat and she was unable to speak.

"Are you Grace Jennings, dammit?"

"Yes," she gasped, anger in her eyes.

"Who's this man? Your husband?"

"No, he's my neighbor."

"Well, get enough clothing for three or four days, cause we're going for a long ride, and make it snappy." He pointed to one of the others and told him to go with her to fetch whatever she needed.

"What are we going do with the guy?" the third man said.

"I don't know, but we're not taking him."

Grace came out of the bedroom with a suitcase and set it down.

"I heard you say you weren't taking Delbert, then I won't be going either."

The man in charge walked over to her and put his pistol up to her temple.

"I'll kill you right here," he seethed as he pulled the hammer back until it clicked into the open position.

"I don't think so, 'cause if my guess is right, you need me and that's the reason you're here, now. If you don't need me, then you might as well pull that trigger cause I'm not going anywhere without Delbert!"

There was a long pause. Time stood still.

"You've got guts lady," he mumbled as he brought the pistol back to his waist and thumbed the hammer back to the pin.

80

"He'll need to go get enough clothes for the three or four days," she said deliberately.

"You're not in charge here lady. So just quit with the orders! Understand?

"You go with him," he ordered one of the others. "Don't try any funny stuff cause if I have to, I won't hesitate to kill her."

CHAPTER 30

June looked up in alarm at the sight of Delbert being shepherded into the house at gunpoint.

"What's going on Delbert? Who is this man?"

"It's all right June, everything is going to be all right, don't be alarmed. It's not as bad as it looks."

"Hurry up and get what you need," the hooded man ordered.

Delbert went into his bedroom and filled a bag with clothes. June stood in the doorway, watching.

"I'm going to be gone for about four days. June do *not* call the police, everything will be all right."

"Is Grace going with you?"

"Yes, and whatever you do, don't call the police! Do you understand?"

"Not really, but I won't call the police."

The two men ran back to Grace's and jumped into a waiting Chrysler 300, Delbert was ushered into the back seat with Grace, and the hooded man into the front seat where he could keep an eye on them, and they were off.

The thugs had pulled off their hoods before they reached the highway so Grace and Delbert had now seen their faces. That worried them. The third man was following in a black Lincoln.

After they had driven for few miles the man in charge turned around from the passenger seat.

"Have you ever had someone you couldn't cure or help?"

She returned his glare.

"No."

"Hopefully for your sake, it doesn't start now with this person you're going to go see."

They had been traveling for about three hours when Delbert checked his watch. It appeared they were heading to Spokane.

"How many people have you healed?" the man in charged asked almost politely.

"Does it really matter?"

82

"Hey lady, it's no skin off my nose, just trying to make conversation."

Grace, who was beyond fear, and into anger, gritted her teeth and seethed, "You come into my home, scare us out of our wits, brandish firearms, force us into this car to who knows where, against our wishes. And you want us to have a friendly conversation with you?"

His eyes narrowed and he glowered at her, turned around and never said another word until they passed the airport.

"You're going have to put these bags over your heads until we reach our destination."

They looked at each other, placed the covers over their heads and the rest of the drive was in the dark.

Once they left the highway the route was circuitous, and they appeared to stop and go. The men were absolutely quiet. Delbert tried to remember the turns and stops but there were so many he had lost track. After, what seemed like an hour, they came to a stop and Delbert thought he could hear the sound of a small motor humming, probably a garage door, or a gate. The car then proceeded forward for another thirty or forty yards. A gate, he thought.

They heard car doors open and shut behind them. Then the doors opened on both sides of the car they were riding in. Someone reached in, gently took her hand and guided her slowly and carefully from the car. Delbert noticed the more 'gracious' atmosphere.

"Delbert?"

"I'm here, Grace."

The sweet fragrance of Jasmine teased her senses, or was it Wisteria. Roses were in abundance somewhere near and the redolence wafted through or under the white cover she was wearing. Someone loved flowers.

"Please step up one step, ma'am," the man directed politely.

They entered the front room of a very large home or building because she could hear someone talking from a distance and the sound carried without interference. They held her arms at the elbow and ushered her into another room.

THE ENDOWMENT

"We'll be going up a long flight of winding stairs, ma'am, but we'll hold on to you."

"Delbert?"

"I'm still here. I think I'm right behind you."

They reached the top and were directed into a room. She heard the door close softly behind her.

CHAPTER 31

"Take those things off their heads. Who told you to do that for God's sake?" a deep, commanding voice ordered.

The hoods were removed. Grace and Delbert were standing in a large, luxuriously decorated bedroom.

"Wait outside the door," a voice ordered the men who brought them here. "I am so sorry. I hope we haven't inconvenienced you too much. Were you treated all right?"

"Why are we here?" she demanded angrily.

"I assumed by now you would have guessed why you're here, Miss, Miss-"

"Jennings. I'm guessing you need my help, but I wasn't told anything. Your messenger boys just burst into my home and took us at gunpoint."

"I'm sorry for how you were treated. I can assure you I didn't intend for you to be treated as anything other than an invited guest. And you're right, we do need your help and the reason is lying over there, close to death. I'm going to spare you the details because it is for your own good that you don't know the particulars. You're obviously a person of God or you wouldn't possess the wonderful power of healing. Simply stated, we need you to heal the man that is lying in that bed. It is not my nature to be rude to anyone or aggressive, but sometimes life takes us where we don't want to be and we have to do things that make us look bad. I'm sure under different circumstances you would like me, and our family. "We're God fearing people and attend church every Sunday, but you're not here to listen to me boast about my family." His hand gestured them to the man on the bed.

"Will you be in need of anything you don't have with you?"

"No."

"I don't suppose I could stay in the room with you and your-"

"That's correct."

"Very well then, I will be leaving and I must warn you that this room is secure as is the entire perimeter of the house. I

THE ENDOWMENT

know I don't need to inform you of all this because your calling is to save lives, not end them. I will be anxiously awaiting the results.''

She looked to Delbert and told him she was sorry for involving him in her ordeal. He said nothing, walked to the bedside and looked down at a very sick man. The man in the bed was hardly breathing, his skin was grayish and his lips were a pale blue. His arms were at his side on top of the bed covers. He looked to be about 55 or 60 years old.   "What if God doesn't want this man to live?"

"He looks more dead than alive, and we don't even know why he'd dying."

Delbert obtained a wine colored, velvet, cushioned chair up to the bedside for Grace.

"I don't feel comfortable trying to pick him up, he's too fragile, so I'm going to pull the sheet under him so he is closer to you, Grace."

"Maybe you should go to the other side of the bed so he doesn't fall off from the jolt."

She put his hands together on top of his chest, placed her hands under and above his. Grace closed her eyes. The man jumped and rolled slightly, and lay still.

Grace slid down between the bed and the chair to the cushioned carpet. Delbert rushed to her and pulled the chair away from the rumpled Grace.

He was on his knees holding her head slightly elevated. She was breathing. Everything was quiet. Grace moaned, began to stir, and looked up at Delbert. He smiled. She gave an exhausted grin and made an attempt to sit up.

"Hey," a man's spoke out.

Delbert, kneeling, looked up over the top of the bed, and saw the man looking at him, bewildered.

"Who are you, and what are you doing in my room?"

He assisted Grace to her feet and she looked down at the man in the bed, who was still confused, but not yet strong enough to jump out of bed. He lifted himself on one elbow and eyed them as Delbert held Grace closely to keep her upright.

"Where's Giuseppe? What's going on here?" He didn't know whether to be angry or afraid. Two people in his room, no lackeys around, and he was trying to remember why he was in bed.

"How are you feeling?" The woman with the large birthmark on her face asked.

"Are you a doctor? I don't quite understand. What are you doing in my bedroom and who is this man?"

"My name is Grace Jennings and this is my friend and guardian angel, Delbert Blair. We were brought here to save your life."

"To save my life?"

"Yes sir."

He lay back down and tried to remember why someone would need to save his life.

"What was wrong with me?"

"We don't know."

"Do you know who I am?"

"No sir, and we don't need to know,"

"So, you don't know anything about me and you don't want to know?"

"That's right."

He grinned. "Who brought you here?"

"Some men, but we don't know their names."

"Where are those men now?"

"They're standing outside your bedroom door waiting for us to tell them you're going to be all right."

"Would you be kind enough to help me to my feet, uhh... Delbert?"

Delbert pulled the bed covers back and slowly sat him up on the side of the bed.

"Would you mind going to that closet and getting me a robe, Miss? Oh, and some slippers, too?"

They stood him up and, with their assistance he walked slowly to the window and looked outside.

"It looks like a beautiful day out there."

Grace and Delbert saw a man that was glad to be alive. "I'm a health nut, you know and I'm anxious to go for a run. Let's go tell the crew I'm all right and get something to eat. I'm famished! What time is it?" What day is it?" He moved slowly to the door, gathered himself and opened it with all the zest and

THE ENDOWMENT

cheerfulness he could muster. His minions all turned when the door opened and there was their boss, standing on his own, and smiling at them.

They stood, speechless, staring incredulously at the man that had lain in his bed only minutes before, all but dead.

"Where's my wife?" he asked the man who had met them at the house.

"She went to St Joseph's to talk to Father O'Malley."

"You go get her and bring her home. Then he pointed to another man standing by the door. You go tell Maria to fix a big lunch for my friends Grace and Delbert and to make my favorite lunch. Go! Go! Go!

"Come my friends, let us go down stairs and have a nice lunch and talk. I feel like talking. Can you believe that? Well, why would you believe that? You don't know me. I'm a changed man. I tell you, something good is to come of this."

They each took an arm, and walked with him down the stairs and into a large dining room. He guided the two to a beautiful Postobello Couture ponte rectangular cherry wood table and had them sit. He slowly strolled through fifteen-foot high swinging doors, into a large kitchen.

"Oh, my God! Mr. Pastorini. Is it really you? Jesus, Mary, and Joseph. I see you theese morning and I don' see no spark. You face... it look dead, Mr. Pastorini. Now you are more than alive. How can that be?" He kissed her on the cheek and took her into his arms in a loving embrace.

"It's all those Hail Mary's and Our Fathers you said for me, and I'm for ever grateful Maria. We're going to eat outside cause it's a beautiful day."

He whisked the two outside to the ample Marley outdoor chairs. Closer to the house were some beautiful Hampton benches, a Sunbrella, and baby blue deep cushioned Hampton outdoor divans.

CHAPTER 32

Gabriella Pastorini, who had gone to St. Joseph's to talk to the parish priest, arrived home to find her husband's bed empty. She was in a state of panic as she ran through the house searching for him. She couldn't believe her eyes when she saw him standing, STANDING, on the patio. She ran to him, sobbing as she repeated his name over and over, half questioning, and half in awe.

"Dante, Dante, my love. God has given you another chance." She hugged and kissed him, then looked him over from head to toe. "What, what?" She was too stunned to form a question, so she held him tightly and cried on his shoulder.

"I went to see Father O'Malley because you were so, so..."

"Shhhhh, Baby. I know, I know why you went to see him. But look at me I live. Come, I want you to meet the lady who saved my life. She is one of God's chosen ones." They walked hand in hand to where Grace and Delbert were seated.

"Gabriella, I would like to present to you Grace Jennings, the angel God sent in answer to your prayers."

She stood and Gabriella grabbed her in her arms and squeezed her as she sobbed and thanked her repeatedly.

"Where on earth did you come from? How did you know my husband needed you?" She looked over at Delbert. "You must be her husband," as she extended her hand. He shook her hand and started to correct her, when Maria came out with a cart and several trays of food.

"Let's put it on the Lazy Susan, Maria, then you and Albert, you come and have some lunch with these wonderful people you brought to me."

Albert stared at Dante with wide-eyed wonder.

"What's the matter Albert, you never seen a dead man walking?" he laughed and slapped his brother on the back.

Maria had placed all the food on the Lazy Susan and had brought some wonderful Muscat and Malbec wines in addition to the iced tea.

THE ENDOWMENT

"Come to the nice table Maria has prepared and let's eat and be happy." They assembled at the table. Dante seated Gabriella and Grace then he sat at the head of the table as Delbert and Albert joined them.

"Would you like to say grace, Grace?" he grinned impishly. Gabriella looked at Dante in astonishment.

"It's your home Mr. Pastorini, and your family, maybe you should say grace?"

"Thank you Grace. You are correct, I should." He placed his hands together and closed his eyes. "Bless us oh Lord, and these thy gifts which we are about to receive through thy bounty, through Christ our Lord. And heavenly Father, thank you for my life. I promise you here, before these witnesses that I will try to be a better person and to live a more honorable life. Amen."

Tears ran down Dante's cheeks, and everyone else's as well. Grace was respectful, touched by what she had just witnessed.

Delbert felt compassion for the sincerity Dante had conveyed and felt the man had possibly experienced an epiphany. A revelation that Dante was now undergoing that would change him into a new, better man from the one he had been before, whatever that was. They finished eating and Dante went off with his brother Albert. Gabriella received a phone call and went into the house to talk.

Delbert and Grace stood and walked around the beautifully landscaped back yard. They marveled at the variety of roses, Japanese honey suckle, beautiful lilac bushes of lavender and white, which by luck, were in bloom and perfumed the area with their own special sweet essence; a clump of California poppies, bordered by two inch cut pine mini-logs and a very large trellis mired in waves of Jasmine. Rose bushes of every color and size were everywhere.

"You know, Delbert, we don't know anything about this family, but they seem to be just regular people; Rich as Midas but, regular. Am I making any sense?"

"Yeah, I know what you mean. On the way over here I wasn't sure we were going to be making a return trip."

"I think we're on the same page, because I felt the same way. I liked what he said in his prayer, about wanting to be a

90

more honorable man. I believe he meant every word. Either that or he's a very good actor."

Delbert nodded.

Dante Pastorini had come out of the house and was moving slowly toward them, followed at a discreet distance by his assistants who looked a little sheepish.

"Albert just filled me in on how you were brought here, and I want to apologize to you both. It is their job to protect me, but I'm afraid my attendants were a tad overzealous. I will try to compensate you. Were you harmed in any way?"

"No sir."

"And you, Delbert?"

Delbert shook his politely.

"You don't talk a lot, do you," he said to Delbert. "You look 'wind blown,' like you work outside a lot."

"Yes sir, I'm a rancher."

"You too?" he asked Grace.

"Rancher and orchardist."

"Well Grace, there aren't enough words to tell you how much I appreciate what you've done for me and my family. You have brought back to life a different man than the one who lay there dying, and I will forever be grateful. You might say I was on the road to perdition. You were brought here under duress and again I apologize. I know you would like to go home, and in a few minutes you will. I've prepared a small gift for you to take with you along with my personal word that if I can ever be of service to you. Call this number." He handed her a business card, hugged her gently, shook Delbert's hand and returned to the house.

After a few minutes Albert appeared and asked if they were ready to go.

As they passed through the house, Albert informed them that Dante had been ordered back to bed for a rest by his wife, but he had instructed Albert to give them the box he held in his hand. It was a beautifully carved wooden box about the size of a large shoebox. "Please accept this gift from Dante and don't try to return it. Instead, do what your heart dictates. He felt that since you were of God, you would do something worthwhile

91

THE ENDOWMENT

with it. He wanted me to remind you that if you ever need anything, you are to call him at the special number he gave you."

"The man at the door has already moved your belongings to the vehicle you will be driven back in.

"Good luck in all that you do, and, from the bottom of my heart, I thank you for all that you've done today." He turned away, but not before Grace saw the tears welling in his soft brown eyes.

CHAPTER 33

Two days later Bob Dempsey returned from Seattle with a suitcase full of clothes.

"Well, has anything interesting happened in my absence?"

The three were seated at the kitchen table, drinking coffee.

"Well, you had no more than left, when we were abducted by three men. We were blindfolded and driven to the outskirts of Spokane."

"Come on, you're putting me on. No way! You were abducted?" Bob scrutinized her face for deception and then Delbert's. He nodded and smiled.

"Well, it couldn't have been that bad, you're both smiling."

She told him the whole story.

"Pastorini. I think I've heard that name before. I'm not sure there's a connection to a crime family, but you never know."

"Well, as it turned out we liked him, if you can believe it."

"So what was in the box he gave you?"

"Oh my God, Delbert. We forgot about the box!" She stood and hurried to her bedroom, returned with the box and set it on the kitchen table.

"You two birds have no curiosity. I can't believe you let that package sit for two days without looking inside. Whoa!"

"We forgot about it, that's all." She said smiling and the three stared at the container.

"Grace, I have a very curious nature, so please open that damn box."

She picked it up and shook it. There was nothing rattling inside. She set it down on the table. They stared down at the neatly carved box. Two small golden latches held the front of the box together and two hinges held the back. The container was about twelve inches square and at least six inches high.

93

THE ENDOWMENT

" Can we *please look inside?*" Bob exhorted.

CHAPTER 34

A week had passed and Grace Jennings' life seemed normal, for a change, and she was content. She had taken the Blairs and Bob up to Lake Chelan. They had boated up to Manson and done some fishing and Grace got a chance to water ski. Delbert took Bob to the Columbia River where he caught a twenty-two pound Sturgeon just a little below the Rock Island Dam. It was the biggest fish he had ever caught and he was on top of the world.

Grace had just finished adding corn and sweet peas to her vegetable soup when the phone rang. It was her friend Maureen Pierce and she wanted to talk to Grace without her husband knowing. Cameron would be going to the doctor in Wenatchee in the morning and she wanted Grace to come after he left the house. Maureen would call her.

Grace assured her that she would be there with, Delbert Blair, whom Maureen knew, and a man by the name of Bob Dempsey. She would talk to her in confidence and alone if she preferred.

The next morning Grace drove to Quincy, where the Pierces lived. The house was small, and neat on the outside, with a fresh coat of white paint. The Pierces had four children and the three oldest were watching Grace as she walked up to the front door. She smiled and they waved and smiled back. The door opened and Maureen looked past Grace to her car.

"Is that Delbert and Bob out there?"

Grace nodded.

"You children go on out back and play. I want to talk Grace."

"Mom, why do we have to go outside?"

"Cause I'm telling you. Now go on, go on outside and play. Do like I say," she said a little more sternly.

"Oh Mom," the eldest muttered, but they reluctantly headed for the back door.

The room was quiet and Maureen looked serious.

THE ENDOWMENT

"You want some coffee?"

"Had two cups already."

"You know how proud Cameron is, and how he won't accept anything from anyone." She fidgeted with her hands on the top of the table. She looked across the room and her eyes welled. She reached in her dress pocket and pulled out a handkerchief and blotted her face.

"Well, about two months ago he burned his leg at work and he wouldn't go to the doctor and it got infected. Now they told him he had to stay home until it healed. They're not paying his full wages and we're having some money problems. Grace I don't know what to do. You're the only person I know that I can truly trust. I've been thinking I could get a job as a waitress in Quincy or maybe Wenatchee and help, but Cameron won't hear of it. I know I could get a job Grace, and we would be able to pay you back. He'll be back working full time soon, and I would pay you all the money I make. What do you think, Grace?"

"I think Cameron is a very lucky man to have you as a wife. How much do you need?"

Maureen walked briskly to a cabinet drawer and retrieved a small note pad. She came back to the table and showed Grace all the accounting she had done, and the bottom line, what they would need.

Grace opened her purse and pulled out a white envelope and laid it on the table.

"I think this will help solve your problem and you won't have to go to work. I agree with Cameron. You shouldn't be working with these children still at home.

I know you want to do anything you can to assist your husband, but the kids need you more, Maureen. I believe you know that.

Now, if you tell Cameron you got this money from me, he'll probably want you to give it back, and I don't want you to do that. So you'll have to think of something to tell him about how you got this money, something that does not involve me. I'm sorry I can't explain it more clearly. There is one more thing I'd like to do today, before I leave. I'd like to speak with your son."

96

JOSEPH F. MONTOYA

"Grace, you know he can't hear. You'll have to write notes."

Grace smiled, "I'll manage. I'm going to ask Delbert and Bob to join us. Would that be all right with you?"

"Of course Grace. What are Delbert and Bob going to do?"

"You'll have to trust me on that, but I assure you I won't put your son in any danger."

"Can I stay in the house with him?"

"Yes, I may need your help to keep him calm."

"What are you going to do to him, Grace?"

Grace looked straight into her eyes.

"I'm going to pray for him to get well. You probably won't understand what I will do, but that will be all right. OK?

Maureen, don't be concerned about your son. It may look like you should be. Trust me. Please. Now, go get you your son and bring him inside and I'll go get Delbert and Bob.

Introductions were made and everyone spoke to young Alex, who was calmed by the gentle nature of everyone present.

Maureen had talked to him in sign language and he was ready for Grace to pray for him.

"Would you tell him to close his eyes and keep them closed until you tell him to open them?"

She made the motions with her hands and he responded in kind. He was lying on his back on the small divan.

Maureen, Delbert, and Bob were standing close by next to the open kitchen, watching earnestly.

Grace kneeled down in front of the couch and placed both his hands in hers and held them firmly.

Bob had opened a large note pad and was writing what he was about to witness. He heard words come from Grace's mouth, some shuddering, her knees thumping on the hardwood floor. The small boy began to jostle on the divan and then they both appeared to relax, the boy on the couch and Grace slowly relaxing to the floor.

Maureen started to rush forward but Delbert stopped her gently.

"Maureen, wait just a couple of seconds. I think everything is all right."

97

THE ENDOWMENT

The three stood staring at the two. Seconds passed. Alex rolled to his back and nearly fell on the floor, right on top of Grace. Grace lifted herself up into a sitting position and Delbert went to her side.

"Alex are you all right, son?" Maureen crooned in hand signs as she approached him.

His eyes widened and he reached out to touch his mother's lips. At that moment the clock over the fireplace chimed the hour. His head jerked in that direction and he pointed to the clock with wonder in his eyes.

Bob stared incredulously at the boy, and thought, so this is what a miracle looks and feels like. This kid could not hear. This was for real. No funny stuff. She wasn't trying to pull the wool over my eyes. This was an honest to goodness miracle. She really can pull it off. She is a real live healer.

"How long have you been talking to your son in sign language, Mrs. Pierce?"

"All his life. He was born like that and has never been able to hear, until just now."

"So how old is Alex and what grade is he in now?"

" He's eight years old and he's in the third grade."

"Do you believe you have witnessed something pretty special here today?"

"Pretty special? This was a miracle!"

"It just doesn't seem real. Has she done this before? She's my friend, you know. Known her almost all my life. But what she did just now, really takes the cake. I've never ever seen anything like it. We've been worried about Alex and what was going to happen to him as he got older."

She sat next to Alex and he cuddled up to her.

Bob walked to where Grace and Delbert were standing and looked directly into Grace's eyes in astonishment.

"By Job, you really can do it. It's one thing to hear about something that's incredulous, but it's quite another to actually witness it's occurrence. Not that I didn't believe, Grace, but well, it's like watching a magician pull a rabbit out of a top hat. You know it's some kind of illusion, but this is the real thing. By the way, how do you feel?"

"I'm a little woozy, but overall, I'm fine.

"Now, was this a typical occurrence or does it change with the person you're, you're healing, for the lack of a better word?"

She looked up at Delbert.

"He's witnessed all of the restorations. What would you say, Delbert?"

"Yeah, this was pretty much the same thing," he drawled.

Bob searched Delbert's face for a hidden grin or a fleeting doubt and got nothing. Delbert was factual and a man of few words.

"I noticed you said 'restoration', instead of healing, doesn't it beg for the word, healing?" he said studying Grace's face.

Grace looked over at Maureen and saw that she was listening to their discussion. She walked to her side and looked down at young Alex. His arms were wrapped around his mother's legs in a hug. She crouched down and surveyed his face and then looked into his eyes.

"You were a good boy, Alex. Thank you."

Grace stood and peered into Maureen's eyes that were starting to tear. Maureen opened her arms and allowed Grace to engage in a silent embrace as they sobbed happily.

Chapter 35

Grace and Delbert were hiking up to one of the many lakes in the Cascade Mountains in the early evening, carrying thirty-pound backpacks and sleeping bags. The trail was easy to follow and the mosquitoes were abundant and pesky due to the bountiful rainfall that graced the mountains in the early summer.

They both had their fishing poles and were hoping to catch some Rainbow or Brook Trout that the Rangers had placed in the high lakes the previous year.

Their seven-hour trek was in its sixth hour and the trail was starting to level off. The summit was approximately thirty or thirty five minutes away. Soon they would see the lake. They would set up a small camp close to the shore and eat something.

They plodded along quietly listening to the forest's symphony of sounds; squirrels, chipmunks, the whistling of marmots, the chattering of Blue Jays and Woodpeckers, the ongoing hum of bees and the irritating sound of mosquitoes buzzing near their ears. There was also the distinctive odor of skunk, the cawing of the crows and the occasional fleeting sight of a timid deer.

Each lost in their own thoughts when Delbert became aware that the forest around them had grown quiet. He stopped and waited for Grace to catch up to him.

"What's the matter?"

"Listen."

They both stood, motionless, hardly breathing.

"I don't hear anything."

"Exactly."

"What does that mean?"

"Mountain Lion or Bear...maybe?"

"What should we do?"

"Just don't move," he whispered in her ear, hardly audible.

She could hear him breathing, his body had stiffened, she didn't know how she knew, but she did. She too, had tensed, primarily from the fear that had transmitted itself from Delbert to her. This was genuine fear and her heart was beginning to beat like an Indian war drum. It was beating so loud she was sure whatever was out there would be able to hear it. She touched Delbert to get his attention. He put his forefinger across his lips and kept his eyes up the trail, scrutinizing for any movement. She made an attempt to remove her backpack and he quickly stopped her and shook his head. The sweat was running down her back and her Pendleton shirt was saturated. Then, without warning the bushes up ahead, just off the trail, began quaking and separating like some large animal was moving towards them a very fast pace.

"Grace lie down and don't move. Do not remove your backpack and lay as still as you can. Pretend you're dead. I'm going into the bushes a few feet away, but I'll be close by."

The large Black bear ran up to Grace and swiped a huge paw across her back hitting the backpack and knocking her and rolling her off the trail next to a tall Birch tree, surrounded by thick brier bushes. He then, went across the trail and was looking for Delbert.

Delbert waved his arms vigorously and when he had the bear's attention, laid down into a fetal position. The bear rushed up to him and grabbed the backpack with his jaws and shook it and Delbert as if he were a small toy. The backpack tore open and the contents fell out. The bear then grabbed his leg and shook, lifting Delbert off the ground and sending him flying across the bushes and landing hard against a Douglas Fur. He lay quiet, almost unconscious from his contact with the tree. The bear ran to him and pawed at his body as if to see if he would move. Delbert lay still.

The huge bear smelled him and drooled on his face but apparently was not happy with the odor. He stood on his hind legs and growled ferociously, then walked off as if there had never been a problem. The forest was eerily quiet again.

Grace did not move for a full ten minutes after she heard the bear leave. She had lain where he had pitched her, and tried to comply with the order Delbert had dictated. Finally, afraid, she dared move just enough to look over the bramble bush she was ensconced in. It was getting dark and she could scarcely see the trail. Where was Delbert and why had he not come looking

THE ENDOWMENT

for her? She had heard the angry bruin brawling with something and the grumbling, guttural sounds were not the sounds of happy. But why, they had done nothing to encourage this barrage of ugly enrage. She felt confident the bear was now gone. Still, she was afraid to move from her little fort of protection. What if Delbert was hurt badly and was in need of her assistance, what if he was bleeding or worse, what if he was…she couldn't bring herself to think it. She stood and looked up the direction from where the bear had come and looked for any movement or sounds. Nothing. She peered in the direction that she had last seen Delbert go. Nothing. Now, it was quiet. Was the predator still hanging around?

The hell with it, I'm going to look for Delbert and if that damned thing comes back, I'll deal with it then. She walked to the trail and considered removing her heavy backpack, making it easier for her to search for Delbert. She placed the pack by the trail and obtained her flashlight. She could still see well enough without it, but what if the darkness snuck up her while she was busy hunting her best friend. Walking into the brush she kept her head and eyes to the ground looking for clues or signs that he had been there. She moved about five yards to the left and started walking slowly back towards the trail. Grace had gone about ten yards when she saw blood. Kneeling down she put her index finger on the red stuff and studied if carefully. She stood and scanned the area quickly.

"Delbert," she said quietly.

Nothing. Walking to the left she noticed the bushes had been abused and she moved herself towards the rumpled shrub thicket and the disarray on the ground. She was walking to the large Douglas Fur directly in front when she tripped and almost fell against the tree. Looking down for the cause, she saw a boot sticking out of the brush with a leg connected to it and fell to the ground beside Delbert or what appeared to be Delbert.

"Delbert," she whimpered quietly, and attempted to assess the damage to her friend.

The brush on one side and the tree on the other made it difficult to evaluate his condition. He was more on his back than on his side. The backpack was torn and mauled and its contents mostly gone. Placing her knees on the ground and freeing his

102

other foot so they were both together she began to pull him out of the shrubbery, inch by inch.

Was that a groan? she thought, as she kept tugging and dragging this six foot, two hundred pound man, or was it the bear. She stopped and listened intently and he groaned again. It was Delbert. Thank God he's not dead. There was blood on his left leg where his jeans wore torn. She was finally able to free him from the bushes and she stared at a man that was in need of a lot of first aid, She stood and went to fetch her backpack.

She withdrew a large blue work handkerchief, wet it from her canteen and washed his face. He opened his eyes and stared up at Grace.

"Am I still alive?" he asked weakly with a distinguishable smile.

She looked down and tears rolling down her dusty cheeks and she smiled and sobbed.

"You better not leave me all alone up here, cause I'm not sure I know the way back," she teased through her tears.

"Would you help me try to sit up?"

"Should you be doing that?"

"Day light is leaving and we need to start a fire. Could you go find an area where we can gather some wood and set up camp for the night?" She rushed off and he forced himself to stand, His left leg was sore but it held his weight so he knew it wasn't broken. He looked at the tree he was standing next to and knew why his chest was so sore. He breathed deeply, very slowly and then expelled it slowly. He didn't think he had any broken ribs, but it was only a guess. His ribs were very sore.

"Oh my God, Delbert, should you be standing?"

"I don't think you'd want to drag me to the spot I hope you've found for us."

She put her arm around his waste and he took a very tentative step and then another until they reached the spot where they would spend the night.

THE ENDOWMENT

CHAPTER 36

Three days later.

"As you can tell from my build I'm not made for hiking. I know that about myself. That's the reason I declined to go with you. I'm really not an outdoors kind of guy. Fishing from a boat or waterskiing, now that I can handle. Walking up the side of a mountain and thinking I might meet a bear or a mountain lion? Whoa, that is not me. Plus my body wasn't made for that kind of outdoors." Bob said at the kitchen table while surveying poor Delbert.

"All the hiking I've done and all the hiking that Delbert has done, this was just a fluke, it wouldn't happen again for another 30 years, Bob."

"I'm thinking you two are pretty lucky to be here talking to me."

Grace turned toward Delbert, their eyes met and he turned away.

"I would agree with that, Delbert added, the bear must have had a cub or two with her to be so aggressive. At any rate, the fault was ours for being in her way. We were on her turf."

"No broken bones: no ruptured arteries, a badly chewed up leg, a mauled shoulder and some very sore ribs."

Delbert gazed at his coffee and pondered about the question Bob posed.

"Hard to say, I weigh a little over 200 hundred pounds and she picked me up and threw me around like a rag doll. Maybe 400 or 500 hundred pounds."

Bob shook his head and peered at Grace.

"You don't look like you were ever in a tussle with the bear."

"That's because Delbert diverted the bear's attention to himself."

"Or could it have been God's way of saving you for things you are yet to do." Bob stated flatly.

Grace focused on Delbert, solemnly with very little emotion.

104

"I'm not sure God had anything to do with this. What would be his point? To punish Delbert for all the good things he has done to help me carry out his good wishes, to punish me for being the reluctant conduit for him. I believe I've tried to do the things he wants me to do or maybe I'm not getting the correct picture. Maybe what I have been doing isn't what I'm supposed to be doing. One of us once said, 'there's no hand book to follow what I'm suppose be doing.' It's just act and react. I suppose I'm sounding like some ungrateful woman whose shoulder God has touched with some clear picture of direction, which I'm unable to read correctly. I feel like a small rowboat floundering about in an ocean storm. No direction." She gazed over at Bob, perplexed.

"Hey, I'm not qualified to give an opinion. I'm a journalist, I write what I hear and see and try to present that as a picture to the reader. So far, I see an ordinary person with a God given talent, one that is quite extraordinary doing the best she can under some unusual circumstances. I have given that some thought. Should an ordinary person be given such great power or such a burden? Bob's eyes flitted from Grace to Delbert and then back. Silence.

"You've thought maybe Father Flanagan would have been a better choice or Pastor Jimmy Rogers or even Timmy Heflin's aunt. They might have been better choices. But God didn't pick them. He picked you Grace, of all the people he could have chosen, he touched your shoulder and you turned around and, and you've been doing his bidding. I'm sure you don't understand why he's allowed bad things to happen to you or why poor Delbert had to take on a bear. But he must have his reasons."

Delbert shook his head, stood and hobbled off to the bathroom.

"I hope I haven't said anything out of line Grace, cause I have come to think of you as my friends and that's saying a lot cause I don't really have any good friends. This God thing is a little out of my niche, but truthfully, thanks to you I'm getting back into the swing of it. I went the whole nine yards with the Catholic Schools and the wicked sisters."

THE ENDOWMENT

"I have a myriad of feelings, a roller coaster ride, if you will, an exhilaration beyond parallel from being that conduit that God uses to heal people. I don't believe I'm special in the sense that I'm exceptional in some way. I really do think I'm ordinary. His choice was of some one that was ordinary. My mother use to tell me I had a wonderful analytical mind and it would carry me through most any situation or crisis. My thinking is I have commonplace complaints about the situation I'm in now, so I'm taking the good with the bad, but still manage to grumble over the bad and marvel at the good. I have faith that God is with me. He understands, it's me with all the doubts."

Delbert returned from the bathroom and back to his chair.

"Wow, this is some friend you have here, Delbert. I noticed the World Encyclopedias along the wall in the front room."

"She reads a lot."

"This ranch has been in my family all my life and it's all I've ever known. My mother had gone to a University and my father had come here from Yakima, and they started this orchard, this ranch. I went to Wenatchee High School and started to go to Wenatchee Valley College until my mother got sick. I did the housework and my father taught me all I know about orcharding. My mother had purchased those 'World Pedias' for me to study when she had her first bout with a debilitating illness and we used to study them every evening on the kitchen table or on the sofa until late in the evening. It was her way of giving me an education because I couldn't attend college. She was very thorough, she ordered books from her Alma Mater to supplement the 'Pedias.' Before she died she said I had the equivalent of at least three degrees, one being Horticulture."

"Very interesting, so your mother died first and then your father?"

"Yes, my father loved me and he adored my mother and I think he died of a broken heart, my mother was his whole life. I know he loved me because he always said I was like her. 'No sweeter woman than your mother and you're just like her,' he

106

used to say." She placed her hand to her mouth and turned her eyes to the floor, tears rolled down and fell on her lap.

"I'm sorry, Grace." Bob said quietly.

She walked to the door and went outside.

"You know Delbert sometimes I can't keep my stupid mouth from running off."

"She's all right, Bob. She hasn't talked about her mother and father for a while."

"Well, leave it to old stupid here to bring it up."

"Don't worry, she's made of pretty good stuff."

"It's hard to believe she doesn't have aunts or cousins or somebody. Man, everybody has some one."

"Well, as far as I know, she's never mentioned anyone, but then, I've never asked."

"What about her face?"

"What about it?"

"Come on Delbert, I'm sure by now you've noticed she has a birthmark on her face."

"Like I said, what about it?"

"She could be beautiful without it."

"She's beautiful with it."

Bob studied Delbert's face and grinned slightly. "I think I've hit on something here that I better not say, unless I want a wounded bear on me."

"You're right Delbert, she is a beautiful woman."

Grace came walking back into the house and went to the kitchen.

"You getting hungry? I made some beef stew and home made bread, also got apple and cherry pies made, too."

Delbert and Bob sat at the table and Grace placed some bowls down and cut the loaf.

Grace's two dogs came walking into the kitchen, wagging their tails and looking happy.

"Grace you've got company" Bob said smiling.

"Well, hello you two. That's right you've never met my two girls, Daisy and Kayla. June has been taking care of them because I've been gone so much.

Along with Delbert, they are the reason I'm still walking around. That night, the night he broke in here, they heard him

THE ENDOWMENT

and began barking. That alerted June, who in turn, woke Delbert up and he came to my rescue. So they're my little sweethearts."

The two dogs sat as if they knew they were being discussed. They gazed up at Grace with loving eyes.

"Which one is Daisy?"

"The Collie."

"So this handsome Rottweiler must be Kayla." He went to the beautiful black and tan dog. Both appeared to be friendly. Most of the Rottweilers he had ever encountered seemed intimidating. Kayla had a sweet disposition, didn't fit the stereotype.

The dogs allowed him to pet and tease with them. Then just as abruptly as they had entered, they rushed out of the house as though a silent, secret command given by one of them. They didn't give the impression they would be good guard dogs, however they were very friendly and lovable. "I like your dogs, Grace."

"They don't come across as vigilant, but I assure, they read people very well. One time I had man that came and knocked on my door, the two were beyond themselves and barked and carried on until the man got scared and left. I always felt they knew he had bad intentions."

Bob thought he had a lot to learn about rural people, farmers and orchardists. They appeared to be overly quiet, less talkative. Delbert was almost spooky, he was so quiet, yet when he spoke, there was no doubt he knew what he was all about. He was one of those tall, good-looking men who said little, but knew a lot. He was never overpowering, yet was solid like the rock of Gibralter, the strong silent type.

The same with Grace, except for the birthmark on her face, she was beautiful, intelligent, quiet and shy. Maybe, they're quiet because of their life style, Except for her neighbors, she didn't have anyone to talk to and it didn't appear it was necessary to do so. Me, I would go nuts living like this, away from people, At the same time I admire the two for their life style. It's like they know something that people like me don't know, and will never know, and I think it's strange I'm even thinking these thoughts. This is a special lady and the more I'm

108

around her the more I realize this was no random choice. God knew exactly what he was doing when he chose Grace Jennings.

THE ENDOWMENT

CHAPTER 37

Bob laid the Seattle Times down and mentally reminisced the story he had written about Charles and Verna Washburn on Baldwin Street in Everett, Washington a few years ago. Verna had given him a synopsis of her life with Charles and their short life together. The home she and her husband had purchased with a five hundred dollar down payment. They had saved every penny they could so they would have a home they could call their own.

She was 29 nine years old and had two children from a previous marriage, a boy and a younger daughter. The day they purchased the home was the day they were married. Charles Benjamin Washburn had turned 21 the month before. The difference in their ages was not a factor. He loved her and she loved him. He looked at least five years older than his chronological age and seemed more mature. She was petite and pretty and looked more like she was Charles's real age. He was devoted to Verna, and her two children loved the strapping young man. He was determined to be the best father he could be.

The year was 1952 and the Korean War had been drafting young men, and Charles because of his age, and the fact that the board didn't know of his recent marriage. At that time draftees could option into which branch of service they would serve. Charles chose the Marine Corps. Verna wanted to contest the draft because of their recent marriage, but Charles thought it might be a good thing. He would be sending his salary home every month, and there was a $5000 life insurance policy he would assign to Verna. Plus he would be doing something good for his country, and there was a thing that the government was doing for all its enlistees. It was the G. I. Bill and one of the things in this Bill was that the government would help send him to college. They both agreed to disagree and Charles was off to Korea. He never stated openly that he might not come home alive, and maybe it never crossed his mind.

Grace and Delbert entered the room and Bob scrutinized his friends.

110

"I'm glad you're here, I just read a story in the Times about a family I wrote about a few years ago and thought you might be interested in. It was a good story, about a very brave man that loved his country, his wife and children."

"Where you going with this story?" Delbert asked quietly.

"Three years ago I wrote about Charles B. Washburn in the Times and I remember this young man and his family. It was a newsworthy, heart-warming story. Charles received the Medal of Honor, posthumously. Verna Washburn is Charles Washburn's widow and she recently had an accident where she works and is now a paraplegic. I'm not sure I'm in any position to make recommendations for where you should apply your gift, but if I could, I would strongly advocate Verna Washburn."

"I'm assuming she must live in or around Seattle?"

"Well, it's Everett, which is a peripheral city of Seattle. It's around 25 miles north of Seattle. It would be an easy trip from here by car or train. I believe the Great Northern railroad runs right through Everett."

"What do you think Delbert?" Grace asked earnestly.

"I'm with you, no matter what you decide, because it's all about you, Grace."

"Do you still remember where this person lives in Everett, Bob?"

"I sure do, if she lives in the same house and I believe she does, if not, I'll call the paper and get the new address."

"Would you consider going tomorrow and if so, how early?" Grace asked with determination in her voice.

"Sure, the time is up to you two, I'm game whenever you want to go. There's no snow on the passes and we could be there in about three and a half hours. I know you're still a little sore, Delbert. What do you think?"

He grinned and nodded.

The next morning at 6:07, they were off to Everett in Bob Dempsey's 1955 Star Chief, four-door Pontiac. Three hours and five minutes later they entered the Everett city limits and headed to Baldwin Street.

"There she is, the little white house on the right." Bob said proudly.

THE ENDOWMENT

"I'll go see if the Washburn's still live here." He parked on the street and walked up to the front door. He could hear voices inside. He opened the screen door and knocked on the freshly painted door. The house was clean and neat. Some one cared about its appearance. A young Negro boy opened the door and stared out at him.

"Good morning, is this the Washburn home?" Bob said politely.

"Yes sir, it is," the young man answered, his brow furrowed in puzzlement.

"My name is Bob Dempsey. You may not remember me, but if memory serves me right you would be Desmond?"

"Des, let Mr. Dempsey in," Verna called from inside.

Bob stepped inside and observed two young men sitting on the sofa. They stood when he entered. Verna, her face illuminated by a huge smile, was sitting in a wheel chair.

" I hope I'm not imposing on something important." Bob stammered.

"Mr. Dempsey," she opened her arms for him and more tears rolled down her face. She looked like she had already been crying. " These two boys were in the war with Charles and came a long distance to see me."

Bob hugged and kissed her on the cheek and then extended his hand to the two men in the room, and then went to Desmond and hugged him.

"I think I remember you two from the dedication the Mayor had for Charles a few years ago, but I don't recall your names. I'm Bob Dempsey."

"Henry Silva, sir."

"Dillard McQuay, sir."

"Hey, cut it out with the sir, you guys are making me feel either old or important, and I'm neither."

"How come you come to be here, Mr. Dempsey?" Verna asked.

"I saw it in the Seattle Times, Verna, you're an important person. I'm surprised the Mayor isn't here."

"He doesn't live here anymore, he moved to some town in California a year ago."

Bob looked at Henry Silva.

112

"Read it in the paper, I live in Renton."

Dillard nodded his head.

"I live in Snohomish, and we were just leaving sir."

They stood and each went to Verna and hugged her.

"If there is anything we can do for you Mrs. Washburn, you have our numbers."

Nice to see you again, Mr. Dempsey, we gotta shove off," and they made their way to the door where they hugged Desmond. Lola hurried in from the kitchen and she was hugged too. They opened the door to leave and they met Delbert and Grace coming in. They made their introductions and promptly left.

Inside, Bob introduced Grace and Delbert to the Washburn family.

Delbert and Grace sat on the sofa and Bob sat on a comfortable Ethan Dell chair. Desmond and Lola stood at the kitchen door listening. The front room was small, with two standing lamps, one by the sofa and the other by the chair. Behind the sofa was a picture of Jesus wearing a crown of thorns. Against the opposite wall was a small end table with a portrait of the family. There was a picture of Charles on the wall in his Marine Corps dress blues. Next to the portrait was his Medal of Honor, incased in a wooden picture frame. A picture of either his mother or Verna's mother was adjacent to the Medal.

"I'm in a little trouble Mr. Dempsey, I'll be getting my last check next week and then I won't have anything coming in. The Hotel is not accepting any responsibility for my accident."

"Doesn't sound good."

"I'd like to be able to get a lawyer to represent me, but I don't have any money."

Lola, rushed from the kitchen and knelt at her mother's feet, put her head on her lap, and sobbed "Momma, are they gonna split us up?"

"There was a social worker here the other day and she was suggesting all the possibilities of what might happen because of my inability to work. Thank God, for the life insurance that Charles had from the Marine Corps, cause it paid off the mortgage. So, at least the house is paid for, but we still gotta eat and pay the monthly bills. The children still gotta have clothes and shoes."

" Then, there are the doctor bills." Verna put her hand to her face and sobbed. "I'm sorry Mr. Dempsey, I'm probly making you feel bad, and you didn't drive over hear to listen to me complain about my problems. Lola honey, go get your momma some water and make a pot of coffee for our guests."

Lola stood, wiped her tears with the palms of her hands and walked to the kitchen. Grace followed her.

"Would you like me to make the coffee, Lola? I make a great pot of coffee."

Lola looked up Grace, then rushed to her and put her arms around her.

"I'm so afraid," She cried as she held tightly to Grace. They rocked quietly, embraced.

Verna watched from her wheelchair as her daughter hugged Bob's friend and she wiped her face with her hands. She released the brakes on her mobile chair and wheeled herself into one of the bedrooms and after a few minutes came back carrying a plastic bag with a newspaper inside.

"I still have the newspaper from when you wrote about my Charles, Mr. Dempsey." She handed the plastic bag to him.

Bob took the paper out of the bag and unfolded it. The beginning of the article was on the bottom part of the front page and ended on page three. He read it slowly and had to extract a handkerchief from his rear pants pocket to keep the tears from spilling on Verna's keepsake paper. Desmond quietly left the room.

"Thank you Verna, it was a wonderful *sad* story then and it's still a wonderful story now. Even, if it was me that wrote it."

"He really was a special person, Mr. Dempsey. Do you know that he was nine years younger than me when we was married. And me with two little ones and he still married me and took on my children, like they was his own. He wasn't much older than Desmond."

Bob studied her face, her graying hair, and saw the strain of taking care of two kids in her eyes. Even now her face showed more optimism than sadness. She was strong and

114

courageous and she exuded confidence under the cloud of doubt and despair.

Bob pulled a bulging envelope from the inside pocket of his jacket and handed it to Verna.

"What's this Mr. Dempsey." She peeked inside. "Oh, Lord, no sir. I can't take your money Mr. Dempsey. My God, no I can't take this money. Thank you, but I can't take it." She shoved the envelope back in his hand.

Bob surveyed her face and knew she meant what she said. This was a proud lady with scruples and dignity and she would not accept this money unless it was presented properly. He knew he had handled this wrong and now, how to fix it.

Grace came in with three empty cups and Lola followed with the fresh pot of coffee. She poured and they sat quietly.

"Desmond, honey, come on in here and bring your momma some of those cookies you made last night."

"Momma," he whined. It wasn't manly to bake cookies and he didn't want anybody to know that he was a good baker. Nevertheless, he trudged into the kitchen and returned with a large basket of peanut butter cookies.

They all took one and then Grace took a second.

"I believe these are better than the ones you make, Delbert?"

"You make cookies, Delbert?" Desmond asked smiling.

"He bakes the best apple pies, and his pound cakes are to die for."

"All right, Delbert!" he beamed as he shook his hand.

"Now you two kids go on to your room and let us talk here," Verna requested.

The four adults sat, and drank coffee and ate cookies.

"She won't take the money, Grace." Bob said stoically.

"I'm sorry Mr. Dempsey, I can't take your money, it wouldn't be right. I hope that won't make you mad at me, but I couldn't pay it back in my condition."

"Verna, the money doesn't belong to me. It belongs to Grace, she thought since you didn't know her, you might accept the money from me."

"Miss Grace, why would you want to give me money, I don't really know you and it don't seem right to take money

THE ENDOWMENT

from a stranger. I know you know Mr. Dempsey, and he's a mighty nice man, so you must be all right, but it jus' don't fit right."

"Momma, Miss Grace is good. She's a good person. I know that about her, "Lola said emphatically from the door way. She walked over to Grace, sat beside her and held her hand.

"Mrs. Washburn that money was given to me by a very generous man. He did not stipulate what I should do with it. I know I don't know you well, but the little bit I do know, and from what Bob has said, I know I like you. You are in need, and right now, I have the ability to do something about it. Please, let us help."

"What if I'm not able to pay it back?"

"You don't have to pay it back."

"I don't understand nobody just gives money away."

"I understand your concern. I'm sure I would feel the same way, if someone presented the same circumstances. In fact, I did when it was presented to me. The man who gave it to me said I would know what to do with it, now, I do. I assure you there is nothing underhanded about it. You won't have to sign anything. You never have to tell anyone you received any money. You'll probably never see me again after today."

Bob pulled the envelope out again and extended it to Mrs. Washburn.

Verna stared at Grace and then Bob, then Delbert. Desmond had come out his room and was leaning against the doorframe. Lola was weeping silently staring at her mother, hoping she had made the right decision.

She accepted the manila envelope. "How much money is in this envelope?"

Grace stared back at Verna and said nothing.

"Please, I need to know, cause I want to pay it back, please."

The room became so quiet they could hear a wind up clock ticking in one of the rooms.

"$5,000 dollars," Grace said quietly.

Verna's couldn't speak. Lola hugged her and they cried together. They weren't alone. There wasn't a dry eye in the house.

116

Verna raised her head.

"Charles did you hear that? Lord almighty, thank you, thank you. Grace may God's love shine on you forever."

"Thank you, thank you, Mr. Dempsey, Thank you Mr. Delbert. Heavenly father, thank you."

"There is one more thing Verna, and it is strictly up to you and you alone," Grace said as she look directly into her eyes.

Verna stopped rocking in her wheel chair and stared back at Grace. The hammer was going to fall now. This money was too good to be true. She knew better than to believe what sounded too good to be true. Grace could see the doubt in Verna's face, the crumbling of hope in her eyes.

"She wants to pray with you, Verna and she needs your consent. God has given her the gift of healing and she would like to attempt to heal you, through God's grace. Now, if you're not comfortable with this, then we'll leave now. We won't take the envelope. As she said, it's up to you," Bob said sincerely.

Verna stared at the three adults and then at her daughter. She didn't say a word, just unlocked the wheelchair brakes and wheeled herself into her bedroom.

The three sat in silence for ten minutes, then Grace, Delbert, and finally Bob stood. They all hugged Lola and Desmond and walked out the front door.

Bob had driven for only two blocks when he turned his car around and went back to the Washburn's. Without saying a word he walked to the door and knocked, the door opened, then he disappeared into the house.

Grace gazed out her back seat window. Delbert stared solemnly out the front window of the car. No one spoke until Bob came out of the house in a full smile. He approached the car.

"Your presence is requested Grace and Delbert is to assist you. I have been allowed to observe. So let's do it."

CHAPTER 38

Grace had received a call from a Mrs. Conrad K. Frizzel about her husband who had a viral infectious disease, called Poliomyelitis, Polio or Infantile paralysis. She had heard through the grapevine that she, Grace Jennings, was able to heal people.

Her husband taught at the local High School in Ephrata. Her request to Grace was that she be allowed to drive down to Palisades and confer with her. Mr. Frizzel was not a good distance traveler.

Grace had asked her if it was essential that they meet face to face. Mrs. Frizzel had stated that her husband would consider the meeting, by his wife, a necessary prerequisite to his meeting with Grace. Grace was aware that Mrs. Frizzel wanted to come and verify she was authentic, not some crackpot.

"What if I was to meet you some place in between Ephrata and Palisades?"

"You would do that Miss Jennings?"

"Your husband is not a good rider, as you stated?"

"Why, yes, that's right."

"As a matter of fact, Mrs. Frizzel, I will come to Ephrata to the place of your choice and see you and your husband personally, with one stipulation."

"Ah, well. You would drive all the way to Ephrata to see my husband?"

"I would."

"I see, and what would that be?"

"I have a very good friend that has escorted me to all the places I've been lately, and I must insist that he be with me. Also, the Seattle Times has assigned a newspaper reporter to write about the 'Endowments' I am performing. So you would be approving the attendance of these two men. You may take as long as you like to consider this offer, but this request must be met as stated."

"Could I ask the name of the reporter?"

Grace handed the phone to Bob.

118

"Hi, Mrs. Frizzel. My name is Bob Dempsey and I write a column for the Seattle Times. I'm on leave of absence, while I'm working with Grace."

He gave her the outside number of the Times and the name to verify his employment. She thought she had enough information and would get back to Grace as soon as she could. She thanked him and hung up.

"She's certainly has some doubts about your authenticity, "Bob said scratching his head. I think I can understand her apprehension. There are a lot of words said, and printed that have very little validity."

"How much credence did you place on me the first time you heard about me?" she asked Bob teasingly.

Bob nodded and smiled wryly.

"You're right. I thought of the illusionist, smoke and mirrors, slight of hand. Even thought of some of the evangelists who supposedly heal people. I'm not saying they don't have some healing abilities, but some that I have seen are pretty hard to believe. The Taro cards, you know what I mean. But now that I've seen you in action, I'm a believer. You have no agenda, you're not selling anything, or pushing a product. That's the beauty of what you're doing."

"That brings up a question, one I've considered but never voiced. IF you were me, how would you go about doing what you think God wants done?" Grace asked.

Bob thought about it, as he pursed his lips and bounced his knees up and down on his toes.

"Well---God didn't pick me."

She gazed at Bob, making him respond again.

"Come on Grace, he didn't pick me because…well, I'm not as even minded as you. In fact, my purpose might even border on the more sinister. Maybe I would try to manipulate this power into some money scheme. I'm not sure I could be trusted with something so right. I'm worldly, more materialistic. Well, you get the idea. I'm not the guy you would give this kind of gift to and hope he did the right thing with it. The more I think and talk about this thing the more apparent it becomes, why you were chosen, Grace."

THE ENDOWMENT

"Grace you're perfect for the job; you have the consummate credentials. You're solid, you have enough resources, through your father's good accounting, you're beautiful without changing what most woman would change if they could. You lead an unpretentious life style and work diligently at farming and growing fruit. You love animals and----."

The phone rang. Grace walked to the kitchen and answered it.

CHAPTER 39

"Well, I guess we'll be going to Ephrata this Saturday to meet the Frizzel's."

"What's his problem?" Bob asked curiously.

"Polio. I had a classmate with it. He had to use a cane and wear a brace on his leg. After I got to know him I wanted to understand better so I looked it up in the encyclopedia. I found it manifests itself differently in different people.

"Hey, Grace you're pretty hip," Bob said with a big smile.

"Not really, but I do read a lot. And these 'Pedias' are a treasure grove of information; the only problem is the minute you buy them, they're outdated. By the way, do you want me to drive to Ephrata Saturday?"

"I'm on the Times payroll, so we can put this trip on my tab. Would you hand me the map, please? The thing about Washington State is that almost all of the names are American Indian."

"Yeah, and that's about all that's left of the American Indian, their wonderful names," Delbert growled.

Bob and Grace turned to look at Delbert. Grace knew that he had a soft spot for the Native American. He had on one occasion spoken vociferously of the indignities and maltreatment the Indian had suffered under the disingenuous American Government. She was aware that the one subject that could catapult Delbert out of his chair was the treatment of the Native Americans. Bob was genuinely surprised by the display of emotion. He hadn't seen this from Delbert in all the time he'd known the quiet, gentle man. It was nice to know he harbored some fire under that calm exterior.

Bob also knew that Delbert had a devotion to Grace that bordered on love. That's what it was all right. Once before he had thought that love had something to do with this man and woman. But does *he* know he loves her? Does *she* know he loves her? Does she love him? Wait a minute, what am I doing?

Bob took out his note pad and began writing.

"Grace, what does this man do? His vocation?"

121

THE ENDOWMENT

"He's a high school general science teacher."
He put his pad back in his shirt pocket and stood.
"I'm going to take a nap."

CHAPTER 40

The man that stood in front of Bob Dempsey was of medium height, wearing a light brown summer suit and soft yellow flowery tie. His hair was short and combed to one side, parted on the left, a small button nose, and a cheery, toothy smile.

"I'm looking for Mrs. Grace Jennings." He extended his hand out to Bob. He reluctantly took his hand. " Well, she does live here, but she isn't here right now, and I can't rightly allow you in because I'm a guest here myself."

" Would it be all right for me to wait in my car until she arrives?"

Bob nodded and closed the door.

Grace and Delbert arrived and Bob could hear the man talking to Grace and Delbert as they walked toward the house. Bob opened the door and was promptly introduced to Pastor George John Jefferson, the Evangelist from the Heavens Gate Revival Mobile church. They gathered in the front room and sat.

The preacher proposed that Grace come to his church and do the thing she knew, which was healing and he would pass the word around to the general public that they could bring their sick to be healed through Grace, who was doing God's work.

"If you really are a healer, blessed by the hand of God? It is your duty to heal?" the preacher stated.

"Why should I heal at your church? " She asked sincerely.

" Because you can and I'm inviting you to our church. Have you ever been invited to a church to heal?

She shook her head.

"Mrs. Jennings you have been given the power to do the things God wants you to do. You have been blessed. You didn't ask to do these miracles. Your name will be associated with God and you'll be famous, even if you don't want to be. Your thanks will be in the message of healing people that can't walk, or see, or talk, or move." *He turned to her and stood, calculating his words carefully. He knew she was considering every word.*

123

THE ENDOWMENT

His wife had always told him it was more effective to say less than too much. He was talking to a woman with a birthmark on her face. A minor flaw, but she was strong and strong willed, he thought.

"God didn't bless you with this power, and that's what it is, just for you to sit on it! No ma'am! He meant for you to heal and heal."

Suddenly, he stopped and reached inside his suit coat, pulled out a handkerchief and wiped his forehead. He was preaching and he had to stop. His wife's words suddenly echoed in his head.

"Miss Jennings, I know you'll think about it. I believe God sent me down here today to see you and ask for your help in preaching Gods word. Your gift has the hand of God on it, and you will be doing what he is asking you to do. You think about it."

She stood, and extended her hand, he took it in both of his and squeezed it gently. Then he walked to Delbert and shook his hand emphatically and then to Bob whom he hugged, turned and exited the house.

"Whew, that's the first time I ever talked to one of those tent preachers. They're quite compelling," Bob said excitedly.

124

CHAPTER 41

Grace walked into the kitchen and emptied the coffee pot and threw out the old coffee, and started a fresh pot. All the time she was thinking about what the preacher had said.

"What's your take on our preacher man, Delbert?"

He stood and stepped into the kitchen and stood against the counter facing Bob and Grace.

"I know very little about the ways of tent preachers, but I have heard they are pretty emotional, a lot like Elvis Presley, when he sings. That's about all I'll say about the man and his church. Not my kind of church, but that's up to Grace."

"Well, it's true no one else has asked me to their church, and he did give me this special talent and I believe he gave it to me because he wanted me to use it. We are all God's children, are we not?"

"He didn't explicitly tell you to go to the Heavens Gate church to heal, though." Bob volunteered.

"That's the problem. I know I've said this before, but there's no handbook to tell me what to do, so it's *our* decision. It's up to *us* to decide what to do. You two are part of this. At least, I hope you're going to be part of the decision making from now on. This is too big for me to determine all by myself. I desperately need you two to help balance everything out. I guess the question I need to ask now, is, should I go to Heavens Gate and heal people?"

Delbert fixed his eyes on Grace and said, "What ever you decide to do, I'll be there beside you and I'll always cover your back. It's your show, Grace."

"I agree with Delbert, it is *your* show, your doing all the work, all I'll add to that is, if you start healing people at the Gate tent, John George Jefferson will have to buy a bigger tent and you will increase his congregation by at least two fold, probably more. My question is. Is he in this just for the money?"

She nodded.

"There is just one other thing I would like to bring up, and it's just an idea, maybe not a suggestion, even. What about people that aren't healable in the sense of broken body parts or diseases or mental problems, what about people that are having trouble putting food on the table, clothes on their backs, a place to live in, what about those people? Like the family you helped in Everett, you gave them money because that's what they needed." Bob stated flatly

"I thought the churches and private citizens did that sort of things now," she said thoughtfully.

"There is always some slippage through the cracks, people that that are forgotten, especially when money is involved. It's true churches do obtain and distribute clothes and food to those in need." Bob asserted.

"Maybe the good preacher does that now," Del uttered.

"We might have to talk to Mr. Jefferson about that. So, is it final? Do we talk to the preacher?" She asked dubiously.

CHAPTER 42

Friday

Grace called the number on the card Mr. Jefferson had given her and made arrangements to meet at the tent on Grant Road. The three arrived early and walked up to the tent where there were workmen moving chairs and working on the sound system. The tent was bigger than it looked from the road.

"Can I help you folks?" a worker asked politely.

"We're here to meet Mr. Jefferson, we're early."

The man scrutinized Grace openly and without discretion until Delbert stepped in front of Grace.

"Is there a problem?" he said directly frowning at the man,

"Oh, I'm sorry, no, I don't have a problem." And he walked away.

They sat in the back on folding chairs and checked out the tent.

The tent itself was almost square, with large metal posts on the four corners. It rose twenty feet or more off the ground with a thirty-foot post in the center. It was a thick white canvas, probably made just for the church. Directly in front of a section of chairs was a stage, that was a work in progress, with several microphones and lines running off the stage to a hub near the back of the tent.

There were several twenty foot wooden posts, with large wattage lamps attached, situated through out to bathe the canvas pavilion in light.

"It's bigger than I thought. Looks like it could seat three or four hundred people," Grace guessed.

"It's pretty big all right."

"Grace, will we be here for all the services? Or just for you to do your, can I call it reviving, instead of healing?"

"Reviving is fine, that's a good question, and something to consider. Maybe, we should mull over the idea of just one day or evening to be here for the purpose of...reviving, right now I don't know what kind of agenda the good preacher has in mind."

127

"Ah, Miss Jennings, Delbert, Bob. I am thrilled to see you and thank you for coming over to talk. As you can see, the tent is a big job to set up, but the people that do it over and over and are quite adept at making it come alive in no time. With the help of God we overcome all the obstacles."

"George."

"Oh, forgive me. This is my wife, Magadalene. Through the grace of God, he sent me the perfect partner. She is the inspiration for all that I am. Thank you Jesus, he said and rolled his eyes up as he hugged his wife affectionately.

"We prayed you would come and at least talk to us about your healing powers, and maybe share them with us. God has led us to your door Miss Jennings. He works in a mysterious fashion. I'm sure you would know that better than George and I. We've only heard by way of the grapevine of your gift, which is surely God given, and to be near you is our gift. Just as he picked George out of all those who would preach his word he sent you to us. Thank you Jesus."

Magdalene turned to face Grace, "I'm sure you are all Christians and have taken Jesus as your personal savior," she trilled.

The three stood, dumbfounded by the statement she had just made.

George saw the moment was awkward and spoke up.

"We're all children of God. Some of us are just more intimate with him than others.

There was silence.

"How often do you hold your services, and what kind of agenda do you follow?" Grace asked breaking the silence.

"Anytime, of course? I think Sunday would be the best time to use your gift. Would that meet with your approval? If not, then you can dictate to us when you would be available. What ever works for you, is what we're prepared to do.

"Mr. Jefferson, Sunday sounds all right to me, but we work as a unit and this will require some conference between the three of us. This is Friday, and we would be able to get back to you by the early part of next week. Do you currently have a specific part of your service when you heal people?"

He looked at his wife and she swayed her head to one side and lifted her shoulders, indicating, whatever he says.

"Now, it is towards the end of our services on Sunday. If it's all right with you we could leave it there."

"Do you have multiple healings simultaneously or do you do each one individually?" Bob asked.

"We've done both. So it is all right with us what you choose to do."

"I've never had the opportunity to do more at one time."

Grace peered at Delbert questioningly at the thought of doing more than one healing at a time. Maybe this was not such a good idea. I'm feeling tentative about the whole thing now, she thought. *Doubt crept in. What if I'm not able to heal some of the people? What if God is opposed to this kind of healing? What then?"*

Bob sensed the apprehension in Grace's eyes and body language. "We need to talk among ourselves before we decide what, how, and if we can do this thing with your church, Mr. Jefferson."

"That's great Bob, cause we're in the same position. We'd like to put a picture of Grace in the paper along with a little background, maybe do some fliers to post around here and some of the adjacent towns."

"I'm sorry Mr. Jefferson. I would prefer if you didn't take a picture of me. You may do a small background, but no picture, please."

"OK, sure. We don't have to take a picture. Right Magdalene? A short background bio will be just fine," Jefferson agreed.

"You can write what you like about yourself and give it to George or me, and we'll put it in the paper and on our flier. All right?"

"By the way, you can dress in any fashion that you're comfortable in wearing."

"Thank you Magdalene and George. We'll discuss the details of the healing process with you later. If we have questions we'll call the number you gave us," Bob stated politely.

THE ENDOWMENT

The three shook hands with the Jeffersons and began their exit from the large white canvas shelter. Outside they walked quietly to the car, but the questions were bubbling inside Grace.

CHAPTER 43

"George, I believe Grace was having second thoughts about coming here. Did you sense that?" Magdalene asked anxiously.

"She's a quiet and introversive person Mag. She was probably overwhelmed by the stage and the thought of healing someone in the presence of all the people on the congregation. Maybe hadn't considered it to be the spectacle that it is. Standing in front of two or three hundred people can be very intimidating."

"The birthmark on her face doesn't seem to be a problem for her, though. I felt she was unconscious of the purple stain on her face."

"I agree. And she appears to be a person of her word. I think you can go to the bank on her word. She'll show up and do what she's been blessed to do. God picks people that don't appear to be what they are. But you and I know better, Mag. God knows what he's doing! Let's not second guess this blessing."

THE ENDOWMENT

CHAPTER 44

"Grace, are you all right with this whole thing, " Bob asked as they traveled down Highway 28 to Palisades.

Grace thought about the question and was aware Bob had noticed her apprehension in the tent. She did have doubts about what she would be doing. Three days earlier she never would have considered doing what she was now inclined to do. Up to now she thought only of healing people in the enclosure of their own homes or at least in a more private confinement and never in some tent where hundreds of eyes would be focused on her.

Could she do this? She knew the consequence of healing en masse and all the exposure she would be receiving. Would she be able to continue to live the life she had always known? What about poor Delbert and June? How would they handle all of this exposure?

Delbert never complains, just goes along with everything I do, whether it's wrong or right. Will I have the opportunity to work my orchard when I need to be there? What about my dogs and my other animals; my little ranch?

She watched the Columbia River moving swiftly down towards the Rock Island Dam, and thought of the song 'Ole Man River.' 'He just keeps rolling along.' No worries, no one to answer to, just keeps rolling along.

"Not completely Bob, but I think we have to give it a try. This church is not my first choice to heal en masse, but they were the first to ask. I believe Jesus would have done this himself, so who am I to question. I don't know if our evangelist is sincere, but I feel we must give him the benefit of the doubt. We can always walk away from it."

He nodded.

"Have you considered how you're going to accommodate more than one healing at a time?"

"I've been thinking of holding hands or touching one another, depending on the count, and while I'm thinking of it, Delbert, I would like you close to me when I'm actually initiating the healing, reviving process. OK?"

132

CHAPTER 45

Sunday.

The three had to park at least a quarter of a mile down Grant Road and walk up to the tent. Grace had worn a man's long sleeved white shirt with black slacks, plain black Buster Brown loafers, no socks, and no makeup. She had combed her shoulder length hair into a pageboy presentation.

Delbert and Bob looked the same as Grace, except for the wingtip and Cordovan shoes. Grace had mentioned they looked like the Kingston Trio. As they were walking into the tent, the congregation was singing, "Bringing in the Sheaves," they looked at each other and smiled.

Preacher Jefferson was anticipating their arrival and the minute he saw them he had the congregation close their eyes and bow their head in prayer. He motioned for them to come to the altar.

"Tonight we are blessed by Jesus to have one of his own, blessed by His hand to heal. Sister Grace is on the way to the altar this very moment and we praise Jesus for her coming.

"Almighty God, we praise you and we pray to you that Sister Grace might heal those who can not see, those who can not walk, those whose bodies are gnarled with disease and tortured by sclerosis; those who have problems with alcohol and fornication."

"Lord God Almighty we pray that we will witness your power through your disciple, Sister Grace. Hallelujah, Amen."

The three stood inauspiciously and stared out at a congregation of gawking eyes. Grace was mentally lamenting her decision to be here at this moment. She glanced over to Delbert and Bob and could see the doubt. Their faces said it all, and the pastor could see it too. He rushed over to them and spoke to Grace, then walked back to microphone and plucked it from the stand.

"Do we have anyone among us who cannot walk or has trouble walking? Please raise your hands. Anyone? Don't be afraid.

133

"Do we have anyone here that cannot see or hear? You folks out there if you know someone like that, please, bring them up here for Sister Grace."

The congregation was quiet, everyone was looking for some one else to stand and go forward. There heads turning and surveying the crowd. After a very long minute the preacher spoke.

"There," he pointed to a man standing.

"What is your name sir? I'm sorry, I didn't hear." Several people shouted out the name.

"Brother Dale, come up here with your wife. "What is her name?" he shouted. The preacher walked over to the makeshift ramp where Brother Dale was pushing Sister Sally's wheelchair toward Grace.

All around the congregation you could hear individual, 'Amen' and 'Jesus saves,' as the throng murmured the spectacle. Sister Sally was now sitting in her wheel chair and peering directly at Grace.

Grace was seated in a folding chair, scrutinizing Sister Sally, whose face was wet with tears as she wailed quietly, patting her face intermittently with a small handkerchief.

The preacher raised his hand and the silence descended to a few coughs and sporadic wails.

Suddenly Grace was aware there was no sound in the tent and realized she was the cause of the deafening silence. She was holding hands with Sister Sally and the preacher was gaping at the two.

Grace turned her head to see if she could see Delbert peripherally. He was directly behind her and she saw Bob writing in his notepad. Don't let me down God, she said to herself and then she looked up and closed her eyes.

The tent silenced as if the air hand been sucked out and no one was in attendance.

Grace opened her eyes and found herself in Delbert's arms.

"You all right, Grace?" He whispered in her ear.

She attempted to sit and check on Sister Sally.

Delbert helped her up to a sitting position.

Sister Sally groaned in her wheel chair, her head bent to one side, her husband looking at her from a squatting position.

"Can you hear me Sally?" Brother Dale whispered.

"What happened?" she mumbled, clearly confused.

"You were bouncing in your chair and I thought she had hurt you," He muttered

"Bouncing?"

The throng remained silent and some were standing by their chairs staring at the stage, wondering what was happening.

The preacher was fixated on the two and was unable to speak. He stared first at Grace then at Sister Sally. He was sure he had witnessed a true miracle; now for the acid test. Still he held his hand in the air to discourage any sound.

Grace stood and walked behind her chair, and spoke quietly to Delbert and then walked to the center of the stage.

"Sister Sally would you please stand?" she said in a strong and deliberate command.

Sister Sally put her hands on the armrests of her grey wheel chair and leaned forward. Her eyes on Grace as she inched her body slowly forward, then in slow motion using arms and legs to a vertical position. She stood tremulously, tears rolling down her face without shame and smiling, yet, grimacing.

Grace was standing approximately ten feet away and she opened her arms out to Sister Sally.

Brother Dale, her brother, now stood next to her and clasped her arm.

"Stand away, Brother Dale," Grace demanded.

Sister Sally took a wavering first step and stared dubiously at Grace.

Grace motioned with her hands to her body for Sister Sally to come forward. The next step was more willful, as she progressed precariously to Grace's open arms.

The congregation erupted with applauds and praised Jesus and hugged each other, folding chairs falling over and collapsing as the assemblage cheerfully fellowshipped and danced their praises to God.

Grace held her hands up, asking the flock for quiet.

The preacher also raised his hand to silence the worshipers and when they were once again quiet Sister Sally gazed down at the deck shoes she always wore and walked over to her wheel chair, then continued to the ramp and down to where it met the canvas-covered ground. She stopped and ran slowly up the ramp and all the way to where Grace was standing.

The worshipers erupted in cheers again and this time there was dancing in the aisles.

CHAPTER 46

The drive home was quiet, everyone lost in thought. Bob was making notes, trying to put into words all that had happened. Delbert was concerned by a subtle change he thought he saw in Grace, and she was simply exhausted.

"Was there something...different today, Grace?" Bob inquired.

"No, I don't think so. Did it seem different to you, Delbert?"

"I'm not sure. There was something. It was kind of like you were barking out orders, or something."

Bob thought about that for a moment, "You're right Delbert, it did have that feel, now that I think about it."

"I must confess I did freeze up when I was standing in front of all of those people. My involvement with Pastor Jefferson and his style of preaching made me uncomfortable, too much like a sideshow. But then, this is grass root preaching. This is the way Jesus would have preached. Remember he was angry with the merchants in his father's house and overtly displayed his angst. I don't think I can fault the style of preaching that Preacher Jefferson expounds. It is definitely grass roots and it has a flamboyant flair about it. I think I felt some of that resonance the good preacher expounds."

There was quiet for a few seconds. Then Bob spoke up. "Quite frankly, I expected more people to come to Grace for aid, especially after the way Pastor Jefferson introduced you. It didn't seem logical to have only Sister Sally come forward."

"Maybe they were waiting to see how it went." Delbert surmised.

" For all they knew, she could have been a shill."

THE ENDOWMENT

CHAPTER 47

Monday.

They were still discussing the events of the day before, while eating an early lunch at Grace's. There was a debate under way about whether or not they would go back to the tent service the following week, when there was a knock on the door.

Grace opened the door to a familiar pretty face smiling happily at her.

"Sister Sally?"

"Sister Grace."

They hugged and fought tears as they held each other.

"We came to personally thank you for, for, oh my gosh, I had all the words ready, a regular little thank you speech and now I can't remember a bit of it. I'm sorry Sister Grace."

"Please, I'm not Sister Grace, I'm just Grace, and you're welcome. However, I'm merely a medium through which God…revives, Sister Sally. I'm a servant of God, trying to do what he wants me to do."

"Hi Grace. I'm Sally's brother. My name is Dale. Are you saying you're not a member of the Heavens Gate congregation?"

She nodded. "That's correct, I'm not." Grace stepped back and invited them into the house.

"I would like you to meet Delbert Blair and Bob Dempsey. Delbert is my neighbor, friend and confidant, and Bob is a writer for the Seattle Times. He's writing a story about the gift God has given me."

Everyone shook hands and then took seats in the living room.

"It's a real pleasure to meet you Bob. I've read some of your columns, interesting. I guess this woman could make a good story."

"She sure does, *and* she's for real."

138

"So who owns the fruit orchards we saw out there?" he gestured toward the field.

"I own the ones immediately around the house and Delbert has the small orchard to the north of the other house you saw."

"I'm glad to hear you're not affiliated with the tent church, officially, I mean, or is that presumptuous of me?"

"That's correct, we have no alliance with Pastor Jefferson's ministry. It was our first exposure to the tent church. I must say it was different, and Pastor George is an interesting and appears to be a good man."

"Some of these tent preachers are, by reputation, nothing more than charlatans, masquerading as preachers," Dale gritted through clenched teeth. "However I'm not hear to bury the man, frankly I'm pleased with the results. I was a desperate man seeking treatment or healing for my sister, so I should be thanking the good preacher, which I did. Do you have a foundation that I can contribute to, Grace.

"You mean like a charity."

"My sister and I reasoned you to be honest and forthright when you helped her. From our prospective you're using God's given talent for the good of all. We can't adequately express the gratitude we feel, for how you helped Sally. We're both God fearing and blessed with more money than we need. You will undoubtedly meet people less fortunate than us, financially, and I have every confidence you will use this money wisely to assist those in need.

"I anticipated you would not have tax exempt status, so I brought you a brown paper bag of money." He stood and Sally followed as he ambled to the front door.

"Sorry for interrupting your lunch. We won't take up any more of your time. Once again, we are forever grateful for the miracle you performed for Sally. We will continue to follow your movements through Mr. Dempsey's column. Don't hesitate to ask for our assistance if you need us."

The men shook hands, Sally and Grace hugged and the Winehouse's left.

The trio went back to the kitchen table to finish their lunch.

THE ENDOWMENT

"I should know the name. It sounds familiar," Bob said, mostly to himself.

There was a knock on the door.

Grace opened it to Dale Winehouse.

"For give the intrusion again, I meant to tell you that Sally and I know the Frizzels and what you did for him was why we came to the church, with all the excitement, we just forgot. He's a good friend and he believed you were the real thing. Sally never had any doubts, but I still had some hesitation about you, however, as you can see now, I believe. Sally and I thought you should know that. Again if we can be of any service to you and your friends, please call us, goodbye again."

Grace closed the door with a smile.

"I should know that name. It sounds familiar," Bob said, mostly to himself.

"There is a Winehouse Lumber Company that does business in Seattle and Oregon and maybe Idaho," Delbert said thoughtfully.

"You're familiar with the name?"

"Drove a logging truck for a company that had that name on all its trucks. Course it was twenty years ago. Don't know if this guy is associated with that company though."

Grace strolled over to the end table where Dale had left the brown paper bag. She sat down, picked the bag up and peeked in.

"We'll add this to the money Dante Pastorini gave us."

"Any idea how much is in the bag, Grace?"

"Why don't you count it, Bob?"

Grace handed the bag to Bob and went into the kitchen.

An hour later, Bob shouted out.

"The man is generous, I must say. Philip Winehouse must be a millionaire when he can give you a bag full of money like this and just walk out the door trusting you will do the right thing. Of course, he must also be fantastic judge of character, like myself," he chuckled. "Though I must confess you are easily read, Grace, you have honesty written all over you."

"How much was in the bag?" Grace asked.

The phone rang.

140

Grace listened quietly to the caller for a few minutes.

"We need to discuss this here and we'll get back to you Mr. Jefferson." She was quiet again as she listened.

"I assure you Mr. Jefferson, we will get back to you."

Two hours later they were still discussing whether they should stay for another week at Heaven's Gate or bow out now. Grace felt if they left now they would be missing people like the Winehouse's, who came because they had heard of her through the grape vine, or the flyers Mr. Jefferson had posted on every surface in town.

The one thing they all believed was Pastor George was a good person, with honorable intentions and his church was overall a good thing. There was a need for his particular services.

There was the issue of whether to become 'formally affiliated,' Dale's words, with the Jeffersons, by accepting a portion of the money donated at every service, thereby coming under the jurisdiction of Pastor Jefferson. The one thing they did not want or need was to be under the pastor's authority.

Grace felt it was essential to attend the tent church at least a couple more times. She knew there were poor people attending Heaven's Gate, people who were in need of what she had to offer.

Bob Dempsey suggested they rent a small house or building. They currently had more than enough money donated by Mr. Pastorini and now with the substantial donation from Dale Winehouse.

Delbert thought renting a house or office space for healing was treating the whole thing like a business. Would they be in need of permits, maybe some kind of license? Could they get tax-exempt status? Would they require the services of an accountant? It was all getting to sound complicated, possibly more so than they had originally thought. The disciples never encountered all this stuff, he thought, but that was then and this is now; whole new handbook. A handbook, that's what they needed. But right now they were compelled to acquire the assistance of CPA or a good accounting attorney. He smiled to himself when he remembered Grace saying she needed a medium's handbook. Delbert thought he might call their

141

THE ENDOWMENT

accountant who took care of the paperwork for Grace, Delbert and June. He would know some one! He knew everybody!

CHAPTER 48

"That would be Rufus Applewood, Delbert. He's not only a good tax accountant but he's a gifted defense lawyer, sharp as a tack. Saw his name in the paper the other day, defending someone on a murder charge. I haven't called him in a while, didn't even know he was still practicing. He's getting up there in age."

The three met Rufus Applewood in his office and spent almost an hour discussing their predicament.

"You've heard of the 'KISS principle' have you not? Keep it simple. Just to keep your selves from stepping on the IRS's toes. You mentioned someone you helped thanked you with money in gratitude. Cash I believe. I never heard you say that, incidentally, and I would never mention it again, if I were you. You're not charging a fee for your service and you should never initiate that practice. Bob you would be wise not to mention finances in any way in your articles about Grace."

Stay away from involving the city, state and especially the Feds. I believe in what you're doing Grace, it's good, you have no motives to become rich or famous, but merely to serve God. The people that need you will find you. I admire your path, but I worry about where it will take you."

Applewood's face radiated his sincerity.

He pulled a large blue handkerchief from the drawer in his desk and turned away from the three as he blew his nose.

Bob couldn't help but notice the office was sparse in furniture, though he had all the proper paper on the wall. He did remember that Number's, alias Tony Moreno, had said he was easing out of the business of law. Yet, here he was, enthusiastic and polite talking like a man who loved life and the need for work.

Grace stood and the other two took notice and also stood.

"I believe you have answered our questions and even injected your opinion on some of the questions, which I liked. I guess the rest is up to us to decide what to do. Your advice about city, state and government is excellent and we will apply the Kiss principle. Do we pay you now or do you send us a bill?"

"I am honored to have been able to assist you in some minor way and I will call my friend and colleague, Tony Moreno and thank him for recommending me. If some legal problem arises in the future, I am at your service. There is no bill or charge for my consultation. I should be paying you for giving me the opportunity to feel appreciated, thank you so much and here's my card if you should need me in the future."

CHAPTER 49

The following Sunday the trio had chosen to attend Heaven's Gate Church again. Bob Dempsey had been reticent, and Delbert had argued weakly against going, but had succumbed to Grace's argument that the people who attended the church were God's children and should not be discriminated against solely because of their attendance at the tent church.

They had arrived early. They were seated behind the congregation in the middle of the center row, and were observing the attendees as they walked back and forth to the bathrooms, or wherever else.

Grace observed a woman in men's coveralls with patches at the knees and a safety pin holding one of the shoulder straps, as she approached them. As she came closer Grace noticed she was wearing an old pair of men's brown casual shoes, with the brown shoestrings that had been broken and retied, no stockings. A yellowish white blouse, discolored under the armpits and had obviously been worn for working outside because the ragged elbows were grass stained. The blouse had brown coffee spatter and food stains, possibly tomato or catsup, on the front. The only indication she was a woman was her shoulder length hair. It was scraggily and unwashed. There was just a hint of lipstick on dry lips, and as she passed her pale blue eyes landed on Grace. Grace gasped at the total hopelessness and despair that brief glimpse evoked. She reached in her purse, brought out a white handkerchief and blew her nose.

"You all right Grace?" Delbert asked quietly and put his arm around her shoulder.

Bob had noticed the same woman and felt the same compassion and disgust that Grace had derived. Delbert was talking to Grace when the same woman came walking by with a young girl. Bob stood and followed.

"Excuse me ma'am, ma'am," he finally touched her shoulder before she stopped and gave him recognition.

THE ENDOWMENT

The little girl, 3 or 4 years old, thin and fragile, looked up at him. He saw nothing but despair in those young eyes, eyes that should have been full of life.

The woman showed no emotion, just stared at him through pale blue empty eyes.

"My name is Bob Dempsey and I'm with Grace Jennings and Delbert Blair."

The woman did not react, just kept the same listless stare.

"What business do you have with my wife?" a man about the same size as Bob asked. He too, was dressed in coveralls and heavy black work shoes, a once pale red and white Pendleton shirt that had splotches of oil stains on the front, and a hole where the pocket used to be. A bad odor emanated from him.

"Do you know who Grace Jennings is?"

The man shook his head.

"My name is Bob Dempsey and your name is-"

The man just stared at Bob.

"I'd just like to know your name, sir."

The man grabbed his wife's arm and the three walked back to their seats.

"Did you get their name, Bob?" Grace asked quietly.

"No, I didn't, they were a strange family. I felt like they were void of any social grace. They weren't nasty or impolite or anything. It was like they weren't used to talking to people.

"Would you try again, I'd like to meet this family and maybe we could--"

"Sister Grace, would you mind coming up to the stage? We're about to start with your healing." Preacher Jefferson said through the microphone.

The three walked up the ramp as the preacher was speaking to the gathering. The trio was dressed as they had been the previous week. Grace felt more in control of herself. She was aware some of the individuals who attended the tent services were in need of better clothing.

"Grace, he wants you to stand up," Delbert said in her ear as he touched her arm gently.

She thanked Delbert with her eyes and stood.

"Jesus, we thank you for sending Sister Grace to this humble church and we give you thanks for anything you will do

146

JOSEPH F. MONTOYA

for those who believe in you. Jesus we ask that you bless all your children, that we may praise you until we are in heaven with you. In Jesus name, Amen."

Grace remained standing and waited for the announcement calling for those in need to come to the stage.

The piano started playing, "We shall overcome," and Preacher Jefferson declared all that were here for the touch of God's hand through Sister Grace, should come forward. The multitude became quiet, all gawking toward the ramp to see who was going to be brave enough to go.

The ramp remained empty and the preacher again encouraged those who would be afraid.

"There is no shame to receive God's own hand to the part of your body that is handicapped. Praise God. Please come to the altar and Sister Grace."

A woman and a young man started up the ramp slowly, hand in hand. The woman looked forward to Grace and appeared confident and assured. The young man, in blue jeans and white shirt, appeared to be around thirteen or fourteen, hair combed to one side and glasses. There was a distinguishable smile on his face. They stopped in front of Grace. The preacher stepped next to the woman.

"What is your name, Sister?" the preacher asked.

She remained calm and answered unnerved.

"My name is Wynona Lewis and this is my son, Bruce Lewis. My son is deaf since birth. I pray that Sister Grace can make Bruce whole."

There was a hushed murmur in the flock and the preacher raised his hand to quell the sounds. Now all that could be heard was an occasional cough or sneeze. The folks in the back of the tent stood, trying to witness what Sister Grace was about to do.

Bob pulled his note pad from his brief case and Delbert took his position behind Grace. A large stuffed chair had been obtained for the purpose of seating anyone who would be healed. The chair was positioned so it was facing Grace directly, and she had a similar chair. She sat and told Bruce to sit opposite her. She explained what would happen to him as she progressed with her ritual of healing. She clarified to the mother that her son

147

THE ENDOWMENT

would temporarily lose consciousness, but not to worry. Delbert would check his status.

"Now, Bruce I will hold your hand and then pray. You will feel something go through you and then it will be over." She was over pronouncing each word because his mother had mentioned he read lips.

She took his hands in hers. She trembled and he shuddered slightly and lay to one side, she eased backward. Delbert checked to make sure she was all right.

Then he quickly checked Bruce for the same thing. They were both all right. Ten seconds passed, then fifteen. Finally Grace stirred. She looked over at Bruce and he moved in the large chair. He pushed himself forward and looked around.

"Can you hear me, Brother Bruce," the preacher said through the microphone.

Brother Bruce's smile spread and he jumped out of the chair and screamed.

"I heard you, Brother Jefferson. Mom, I can hear."

"Praise the lord. Jesus, we give you thanks for restoring Brother Bruce's hearing and for Sister Grace.

The congregation cheered and praised Jesus and whistled and shouted, "praise God."

Suddenly, the preacher raised his hands for the assembly to stop all the cheering.

"Brothers and sisters. God is not through healing today. We have another brother standing at the ready before Sister Grace."

Bob recognized the man as the person he had tried to talk to at the back of the church. He was carrying a small child in his arms. The little one looked thin and feeble. He had dark listless eyes that did not see, and his body hung lifelessly in his father's arms. His once white t-shirt was grey and he wore only grey socks and a ragged cloth diaper. His knees showed the abuse of struggling on dirt or a hardwood floor.

'What is your name, Brother?" the preacher asked through the microphone.

The man turned and looked at the preacher.

"Ro Ro...Roland. My name is Roland."

148

"Is this healing for you or your daughter, Brother Roland?"   "It's, it's for my son," he stuttered.

"Praise the Lord, Brother Roland. Jesus we pray that Sister Grace will touch this poor handicapped boy, and with the help of Jesus make this poor child of God, whole. Almighty Father, let us witness your mercy now and let Sister Grace follow your instructions and we'll praise you for your mercy, Amen."

The preacher leaned over and whispered in Roland's ear and then through the microphone he stated the boy's name. The man sat on the chair opposite Grace. His son sat in his father's lap, facing her.

Grace explained to the man what would happen in the next few minutes and then she clasped the boy's feet in her hands. The man placed his right hand on top of Grace's and she closed her eyes.

Quiet took the stage for few seconds.

Grace stood, with Delbert's assistance and eyed the two across from her. The man and the boy both appeared groggy. The boy had slid between the father's legs; his arms supported him from falling to the floor. The father's head lolled back. The boy took two steps backward and was now standing away from his father without support. He walked unsteadily to the ramp, then back to his father who was now fully awake. The boy's mother scurried up the ramp to be with her husband and son. When Sonny saw her, he hurried to her open arms.

"Praise be to God!" the preacher shouted through the microphone. "Praise the Lord."

The mother and daughter were crying, sobbing, when the father joined them as they made their way down the ramp and were swallowed up by the happy hysterical assembly.

CHAPTER 50

The following day as they discussed the prior Sunday, Roland Longwagon called to thank Grace for healing his stuttering problem and for healing their son of the MS he had from birth.

"I got your telephone number from Pastor Jefferson. I hope that was all right," Roland said apologetically.

"It's OK. I'm glad you called cause we, my associates and I, would like to come and see you at your home."

Roland froze. Mr. Burbank, his landlord and employer was pretty clear about not wanting anyone on his ranch, no visitors. "I don't think that's a good idea."

"Roland, do you have a job?"

"Yes ma'am, I have a job. I work as a mechanic and handy man at the Burbank Ranch in Quincy. Mr. Burbank allows me to live in his cabin behind the ranch house and he docsn't like me leaving the ranch when he's not there."

" Would it be possible for me and my two associates to come by and talk to you for a few minutes?"

Roland thought what harm could that do, after all Grace had cured his son's terrible disease and fixed his stuttering. She wasn't asking for money for what she had done, just trying to be nice.

'I guess that would be all right," and he gave her the address.

The drive to Quincy from Wenatchee took the them out of the Cascade Mountains, crossed the Columbia River and ascended a gradual thirty-mile incline until you were on top of a plateau. The land was barren and rocky, but where it was fertile it produced everything from turnips to wheat. A tree in this area was a rare sight until one reached Spokane where the pine trees were everywhere.

"The next road should be Harvest Road, " Delbert informed Bob, who was driving. "We have to make a right."

150

They drove up another couple of miles and they saw a ranch style home on the right. It sat off the road about thirty yards with three red Ford trucks beside a harvester and other farm paraphernalia utilized for planting and harvesting a variety of produce. They stopped at the driveway entrance and checked the name on the mailbox.

"Luther Burbank," Grace recited.

Bob drove the car slowly down the two way blacktopped drive way. A large German Shepherd ran toward the car as it neared the house, barking all the way and then just as quickly, disappeared. A dirt road angled around the house leading to the back. The three exited the car, followed the dirt tracks to a small house about twenty yards behind the main house. A much used repair facility was located on the other side of the dirt road, where Roland probably applied his trade. There were individual tractor parts, truck engines, several tires varying sizes, some new and some flat, and tilling equipment. A tractor engine was hoisted on an engine pulley. There were countless different varieties of farm tools and equipment. Some were in a semblance of order, others strewn about the vast garage.

Roland had seen the three from his small home and came to meet them.

"Good to see you Roland," Grace smiled. The other two stood back.

"It's nice to see you too," he said tentatively.

Grace studied the man curiously and wandered what made him so apprehensive, so nervous.

"Is there something wrong, Roland?"

"Well, Mr. Burbank doesn't like people on his property and he has told me not to have company here." he said as he squinted nervously past her down the road.

Bob and Delbert also turned and looked down the road.

"Would you be in a lot of trouble if he found us here now?"

He nodded.

"Are you expecting him back soon?"

Again he nodded.

"Are you happy working here?"

"It's a pretty good living."

THE ENDOWMENT

"Does he charge you rent for your cabin?"

"No."

"Does he pay you a salary for your work?"

"Miss Grace, I want to thank you for what you have done for my son and for me, but you should go now, before he gets back."

"We've got company Grace," Delbert said earnestly.

"Please go," Roland said nervously.

Grace didn't want Roland to get into more trouble than he was in and she turned to leave with Delbert and Bob trailing.

Roland watched from the garage and hoped they would just walk by Mr. Burbank and leave. He could see Mr. Burbank had stopped them. This did not look good for him.

A large man stepped toward them from the Chevrolet pickup that had just arrived.

"What's your business here?" he asked harshly.

The three kept on walking as if they had not heard the question.

"I wrote down your license number as I came in and I'll call the Sheriff if you don't answer my question."

They stopped and faced a man six feet plus. He was balding and had grey in what was left of his hair. He seemed comfortable barking out orders and expected answers. He had at least a day's stubble on his face, and his face was not designed for smiles.

"We just wanted to talk to Roland for a minute," Grace answered politely.

"And just what the hell did you want to talk to Roland for?"

"I don't think it's any of your business," Delbert said with a hint of anger.

The man stared at Delbert.

Delbert returned the glower.

"I believe I was talking to Miss Pink face."

Delbert made a quick movement to the man, but Bob reached out and grabbed him.

"He's got the advantage here. We're on his property, Delbert," he whispered.

152

"Your friend is right, you have no right to be on my property and I could have you thrown in jail for trespassing, or I could just as easily kick your ass out of here. Either way.

"Roland knows my rules and I believe he has broken those rules. I'll be talking to him after you leave."

"Mr. Burbank, we met Roland recently and just wanted to check on him, make sure he was OK."

"Ohhhhh, he told me about somebody at that tent church, which is nothing more than a circus for freaks that want to believe some insane idea that there is a God and that he performs miracles. I don't pretend to know how you stopped his stuttering, if you have. That remains to be seen. As for his son, he probably just decided to stand and walk on his own. I don't believe there was anything wrong with him in the first place. Roland should believe in himself if he wants to believe anything. I've given him a good job here and that's to be believed. Now before I loose my temper, you three intruders best leave my property. As for you, Miss Pink Face lady, there is a better way for you to make money than stealing from the poor."

Delbert, who was trembling from the rage he was suppressing, stood quietly for a few seconds until his better judgment was squashed into submission by the anger, he ran full force and tackled the arrogant Luther Burbank. They rolled on the ground, then they both sprang to their feet. Delbert threw a hard right to the left side of Luther's face and down he went. From a sitting position, he threw dirt in Delbert face, jumped to his feet and punched Delbert squarely on his face. Delbert fell to the ground blinked his eyes in an attempt to clear his vision. Luther tried to kick him when he was down. Delbert rolled to one side, reached out and grabbed his leg. He pulled the leg out from under him and Luther crashed to the ground where Delbert rolled on top of him and pummeled his face, until Bob grabbed his arm.

"Stop it Delbert! Stop! Stop!" Bob screamed.

Delbert stood up, covered with dust, dry hay particles and blood. He eyes fumed down at his antagonist.

"You, you."

"Come on Del. Let's get out of here," Bob urged.

THE ENDOWMENT

"I'm calling the Sheriff," Luther said as he struggled to his feet.

"What are you going to tell him?" Delbert wanted to know.

"You saw him attack me first," Luther said to Bob.

"Did I?"

Luther turned his head toward Grace.

Grace gazed at Luther for a few seconds and then walked around to the passenger side and climbed in.

Bob turned the car around.

Luther stood staring as they drove off.

CHAPTER 51

Tuesday.

"I'm calling 'cause he fired me and kicked us out of the cabin. We don't have anywhere to go," Roland sobbed. "I don't know what to do. I'm in a bad fix, just didn't know who to call, Miss Grace."

"Where are you Roland?"

"I'm calling from the 76 gas station in Quincy."

"Do you have transportation?"

"We're all in my pickup, but don't know where to go."

Grace gave him directions to Wenatchee and a motel on the Avenue. She told him she would make arrangements for his family to stay in a motel until they could find a more permanent residence.

An hour later the old Chevrolet pickup arrived with the all four of them in the front seat. Grace directed Roland to a parking space.

The manager came out and extended a key to Roland as he stepped out of his truck. His wife and children were quite confused and were reluctant to leave the safety of the truck.

"Roland, invite your family to get out of the truck. You're going to spend the night here."

"I don't understand, who's going to pay for all this? We don't have any money, Miss Grace."

"Don't worry about the money, that's all been arranged. Do you have any suitcases?"

"We just have the three brown bags for the kids clothing, is all." Roland said politely.

Grace made a mental note to take the family to Penny's or Sears for a clothing apparel venture the next day. They were all in need of wardrobes.

Delbert had a friend who worked at a North Wenatchee Avenue garage and knew the mechanic network. He was referred to a garage in the South end of the Avenue. Delbert talked to the owners, Dick and Ray wolf about hiring Roland Longwagon.

155

THE ENDOWMENT

Dick insisted he meet the man and discuss his mechanical background and then he would consider the proposition.

The following day Delbert and Roland arrived at the garage and Roland talked to the owners for about a half. They shook hands and he walked to Delbert's car and told him the owners wanted to talk to him.

"Well, he seems to know mechanics, primarily Fords and Chevrolets which is what I service most, so we're going to give him a try for a week, he'll have to earn his keep, though."

"Thank you Dick, Ray, I don't think you will regret hiring him. Just one more thing, could I suggest you keep him for a month and we'll take care of his salary for that month? We are that confident he will work out for you."

"Well, that sounds more than fair to me, Delbert. A month should tell us if it's going to work out." Dick extended his hand. "It's a pleasure doing business with you."

Bob had canvassed the paper for home sales that were in the price range the three had agreed upon. The Longwagon family had followed the three to all four of the homes and they had agreed with the help of the three to a home that was close enough to a grade school for the children to walk. There was a Mom and Pop grocery store to obtain milk and bread or other essentials. There had been the usual bickering over the final cost of the home and that had been resolved. The papers had been signed, the keys had been obtained and the Longwagon family was finally settled in their new environment.

"I can't believe we accomplished all this in less than three days. I never realized helping someone less fortunate could be so darn much fun. All of this brought to fruition because Grace was literally abducted from her home and then saves the man's life, then rewarded with thousands of dollars."

"Winehouse too." Grace chimed in.

"Yes, and Dale and Sally Winehouse, how could I forget their generosity."

"Even our own Delbert Blair helped to consummate all this, wouldn't you say, Bob?"

"Yeah," he said nodding his head, "by beating the crap out of that arrogant son of...I guess in a way we owe our gratitude to Luther Burbank in some, cryptic way.

156

Delbert rolled his eyes and smiled

"Isn't giving a wonderful thing." Grace sighed smiling.

CHAPTER 52

"Mr. R. W. Newberry, my name is Grace Jennings. You don't know me."

Click.

"What happened, did you lose him?" Bob asked, raising his eyebrows.

"He hung up on me."

"You want me to try?" he said moving over beside her. "Let me try a different approach. Remember what Dale Winehouse said about him? He's suspicious, has a very narrow point of view, and little faith in religion or, in his words 'the God theory.' He's very wealthy and wields a lot of power. Just don't step on his old toes." Bob said as he scrunched up his face in imitation of Philip Winehouse.

How do you help someone who doesn't allow you to approach him? Delbert thought.

Grace picked up the phone again.

"Newberry residence, may I help you?"

"I would like to speak to R.W. Newberry, please. My name is Grace Jennings."

After a very long ten seconds.

"What is this all about, Miss Jennings? Do you know who I am?"

"Yes sir, I do and this is about your granddaughter and her condition."

"Please understand I have friends in high places and I won't tolerate any funny business or any subversive coercions, do you understand? Now, what is your business with me and my granddaughter?"

"Simply stated, I would like to come and see her. I've been told she has Polio."

"Where did you get that information?"

"Sir, I have sworn that I would not divulge that information."

There was a pause.

"Are you a Medical Doctor?"

"No sir I'm not."
"What is your profession?"

She paused, knowing he was *not* going to like the answer.
"I'm an orchardist...a rancher."
"Surely you jest. Did you call me just to mock me?"
"Sir, you asked me a fair question, an honest question, one that deserves a truthful, honest answer. I am an orchardist and rancher, and that is the truth. I understand what you must be thinking. Some nut calling you, wanting to see your granddaughter with some idea of---" He interrupted her, "Are you leading me to believe that you can cure her?"
"Yes sir. If it is God's will. I guess that is what I'm saying."
Click.
"I don't believe it, he hung up on me again."
"What did he ask you?" Bob asked.
"Essentially, he asked me if I thought I could heal his granddaughter."
"Winehouse knew what he was saying when he told you he would be a tough nut to crack," Bog affirmed.
Grace thought about the man and understood his reluctance. She would probably react the same way if some one called and made the same assertion. An orchardist who could heal someone with Polio? What's wrong with this scenario, other than it seems completely absurd.
Bob Dempsey thought about it for a while, and approached Grace."
If I can convince him we have some credibility it might possibly turn him around."
Bob dialed the number.
" Hi Mr. Newberry. Please don't hang up on me. I write an editorial for the Seattle Times and I'm writing a story on Grace Jennings, the woman who called and spoke to you a few minutes ago. She is in fact an orchardist, and I have seen what she can do for people who have handicaps. The point I'm trying to make is that all she's asking is a little of your granddaughter's time and possibly, with God's blessing, make her whole. There

THE ENDOWMENT

is nothing Miss Jennings would do that would endanger her life, and quite possibly, help her in a way that would make you proud and happy. I would also be there as a witness and to verify her special talent. Surely you could give your granddaughter that opportunity?"

There was no sound at the other end of the phone. Bob wanted desperately to say something but held his tongue. Finally.

"What is your name sir?"

"Bob Dempsey."

"I know your boss and if you are lying to me you are going to be in a lot trouble."

"Yes sir, I guess I will."

"Call me back in fifteen minutes?"

The three checked their watches and all agreed it sounded like they would probably get an audience with Mr. Newberry.

Fifteen minutes later Bob called back and was received more cordially, but the skepticism hadn't gone entirely.

Mr. Newberry would invite them to his home but he would query the three a little more definitively. Bob Dempsey agreed and was given the address and a date was set for the following day.

CHAPTER 53

The drive to Seattle was nice except for the rain through Snoqualmie Pass making the trip a little slower for safety reasons. The weather was warm and humid and Grace opened her window to allow the rain soaked vegetation to waft through the car and scintillate the nose. She could smell the aroma of wild Jasmine and Pine. The mixture of all the wonderful smells and the panoramic view of millions of the different types of Cedar, Fir, Woody Cone, Hemlock, Larch, Pine and the beautiful Blue Spruces. Not that she was an outdoorsman, or avid camper, she just loved the eye feast of all the trees she could see going over the roads, both Blewett and Snoqualmie Passes. The hum of the engine, the raindrops pounding the hood of the car, the windshield wipers bumping from side to side, the wind sneaking through the partial opening of the window, created an almost orchestral sound if you listened intently enough. Delbert and Bob were in their own mental world with their own focus and remained silent. She remained gazing at the forest of trees.

The drive to the Newberry home was beautiful and scenic. His home was gated with a large lawn and captivating aspen trees disbursed among a few Chinese and Red maple and at least three gorgeous Smoke trees. The floral landscape was a Van Gogh mural with sunflower interspersed among the wondrous variety of Roses.

Bob parked the car in a circular driveway and the three ambled to the door where a middle aged Japanese woman greeted them solemnly.

"Mr. Dempy."

"Yes, I'm Mr, Dempsey."

She walked ahead to a room and they trailed her down the hall where she opened the door to a small room with ample seating.

"Mr. Nubayee come to see you soon."

The three sat and observed the room with all the beautiful prints of famous painters on the walls. The door opened and a tall man with a full head of gray hair the room. He

THE ENDOWMENT

was dressed a smart blue blazer, light grey bow tie and grey slacks. A very serious face carefully scrutinized the three of them.

Grace thought the man looked like an eagle, a great American Bald Eagle, with an aquiline nose and piercing brown, flitting eyes. He seemed ready to impugn their right to be in his presence.

"Mr. Dempsey."

"Yes sir," Bob stood up.

"I'll give you three minutes to state your case. I'm a busy man."

"State my case?" Bob asked, somewhat confused.

"Your purpose in coming here today," Mr. Newberry barked.

Grace stood and peered at the angry eagle.

"My name is Grace Jennings and my pur---"

"I believe I was directing my statement to Mr. Dempsey," he said, cutting Grace off.

"Mr. Newberry, I can see that you are a pompous and arrogant man and the attitude your directing toward us is insulting. We have driven a long way to help your granddaughter, and you allow us three minutes to state our case? Your arrogance and pride are more important than her welfare? Mr. Dempsey, I don't wish to stay here another minute and listen to a man who does not want to hear our purpose for being here. We are obviously not important enough to be in your presence, and I suggest we leave this…this *eagle*."

She grabbed Delbert's arm and headed toward the door, Bob followed. The three walked briskly down the long hallway and out the front door, without speaking. They got in their car and proceeded to the gate. The gate remained closed and they sat waiting for someone to do something. Bob pushed the call button and waited for someone to respond. He turned and looked back toward the house.

"Maybe we're purposely being delayed for the authorities," Bob said disdainfully.

The three sat quietly and stared at the motionless iron-gate.

Finally a voice purred from the speaker next to the gate.

162

JOSEPH F. MONTOYA

"This is Mrs. Newberry. I would like to apologize to Miss Grace Jennings and her two associates for my husband's rude and obnoxious behavior. I would like to welcome you to come back and listen to what you propose for our granddaughter. However, if you wish to leave, I understand. I will open the gate for you."

The huge gate swung open slowly and the three were free to leave. After a few moments the car backed up to the front door again.

Mrs. Newberry was standing at the door. She was short and thin, but not frail. She had on a grey dress with a single strand of pearls around her neck. A pair of glasses hung from a long cord. She wore her short grey and black hair in a casual style. Her smile seemed genuine. She spoke quietly to the trio as they approached her.

"We have people who speak for us routinely and I think we forget how to talk to other people. My husband is a wonderful man and, as you can see, he has been very successful. Most of the people we deal with are those who want something from us and so we have become defensive and sometimes obstinate. But I don't believe I heard that you wanted anything from us. Is that correct?" She was looking at Grace.

"That's correct Mrs. Newberry," Grace responded politely.

They reentered the room the maid had brought them to the first time and they were all seated.

"Certainly you can understand we are not living in the days of Joan of Arc or the times of miracles, if there *ever were* miracles. God is a slippery slope in our days, wouldn't you agree, Miss Jennings---it is Miss, correct?"

"That's correct."

"If I sound cynical, it is because our world has lost touch with God, and the only god that is pursued nowadays is the mighty dollar. What kind of credentials do you carry that you should know other wise? I believe you told my husband that you were an orchardist/rancher." She paused and reflected on her interrogation. Oh good heavens, I'm sounding like my husband. Please, tell me why you're here and I will listen sincerely. I understand you have come a long way and I will honor your

163

THE ENDOWMENT

sacrifice and hear you out. My tendency is to blither without thought, so I will shut my mouth and listen."

"Does your granddaughter live here?"

"She does."

"I'm not much for blithering or expending extra words. That is **my** way. I will say I did not *request* what God has chosen for me. Personally, I believe there are many more who should have caught God's eye, certainly more deserving. Having said that, I *was* chosen. I'm not sure it's a blessing, even though so far it has been extremely gratifying."

The four just stared at each other and then Mrs. Newberry spoke.

"I think I like you Miss Jennings."

"Thank you. I believe I like you too. Would it be possible to speak to your grandchild? In your presence, of course."

Mrs. Newberry extended her hand to a small plastic box on the end table and pushed a white button.

The oriental maid walked into the room and stood in front of Mrs. Newberry.

"Would you please bring Gilda into the study for me, Yoko?"

CHAPTER 54

A beautiful child, smiling shyly, was soon wheeled into the room. She had curly blonde shoulder length hair that hugged her head closely. Her eyes were deep, deep blue, offsetting her pale white skin. She appeared diffident, her eyes darted to her Grandmother for help.

The wheel chair hid her frail body. She sat motionless, waiting for some direction from her Grandmother.

"This is Gilda Watling Newberry. Gilda this is Grace Jennings and her two associates. They've come a long way to talk to you."

Grace walked to the small child, knelt in front of the wheelchair and gently took Gilda's small white hands in hers.

Gilda gazed into Grace's eyes and felt as if she had known her all her life and smiled widely. She peeked at her grandmother and started speaking with exuberance.

"Sometimes I pretend I can walk. Gram's backyard is full of Lilac bushes, Tulips, California Poppys, wonderful Wisteria, rose bushes that are blossoming and the aroma is heavenly. I pretend I can climb the trees in the back yard. Gram loves trees and has them standing like good soldiers in her yard. She calls them good soldiers cause they never talk back. She has a little group of White Birch, with white bark, a Weeping willow, a tall Canary Island pine, a fluffy English Maple, and several gorgeous Aspen." Tears were welling in her eyes and her voice trailed off as she mumbled the names of the flowers.

Tears ran silently down Grace's cheeks. Grandma Newberry was crying quietly, her head in her hands.

"Would you like to stay, Mrs. Newberry?" Grace asked quietly.

"I thought I would, but now I don't think I can. I'll be across the hall."

Mrs. Newberry sat on a large sofa and looked toward the heavens.

I haven't forgotten you God, she thought quietly. *You've always been there. Though mostly on the backburner I'm sad to say. You made my husband rich and powerful and we forgot where it all came from. I won't be disappointed if it doesn't work out for Gilda. Grace has put you back in my heart. I thank you for sending us this woman, and for making me feel like a---a Christian again. Win, lose or draw, I'm in your corner again, God. I haven't felt---*

"Grams...Grams," In a hushed voice, Gilda spoke from the open door, to her grandmother.

Mrs. Newberry opened her eyes and slowly lowered them to find her granddaughter standing...STANDING in the doorway. She was holding the doorknob, then let go and entered the room. They gazed into each other eyes, never wavering.

"Praise God, child" she voiced and held her arms open for Gilda to come to her.

They held each other, crying softly and rocking back and forth.

Grace, Delbert and Bob walked down the hall toward the front door when they heard Mr. Newberry call out Grace's name.

They stopped at the open door, waiting for the man to approach. Mrs. Newberry and Gilda came out into the hallway to watch.

"It's understandable you would want to leave without saying anything. I was rude and resistant, thank God my wife was intuitive enough to call you back. I surely owe you an apology...and more. Please come back to the study and let us thank you properly."

Gilda ran past her Grandfather to Grace and hugged her tightly.

"Please Grace, they are wonderful people. Now I can show you the trees I want to climb, and show you all the flowers in Gram's backyard, please come with me to the back," and she took her hand and started for the back of the house.

Grace's teary eyes said it all, as she looked at Delbert and Bob.

"Go with her, Grace," Delbert said and Bob nodded his approval.

Delbert and Bob walked back to the study and sat facing the large windows that opened to the back of the house, where they saw Gilda and Grace strolling on the grass. Gilda pointing out which flower was special and which tree was her favorite. Her frail little legs were chicken-like in appearance but strong enough to skip around the very large estate and the marvel at the panoramic beauty.

Delbert took notice of Grace's demeanor and warmth spread through his body. He knew she was special and it made him very happy to be her friend. He had always loved her, but now it was different even though he didn't know why.

Bob took out his note pad and began writing. He had only written a few lines when Russell Wade Newberry, the grandfather interrupted him.

"Mr. Dempsey, your boss said you were a fine and honorable man and that you could be trusted. Forgive me my suspic---."

"You don't have to apologize, sir. We didn't blame you for having doubts. We knew you would be skeptical. God picked Grace with careful consideration. Her will has been bandied and tried, but she does find resolution. She's unselfish, generous, kind, and human, sir, and I respect her. She's not perfect, but she sure tries to be."

"Is she really just a rancher and orchardist?"

Bob nodded.

"Has she ever considered having the birthmark on her face removed?"

"Not that I'm aware. Funny thing about that birthmark, after you're around Grace for a while you don't even notice it."

"Is she an evangelist, or clergy of some sort?"

"No sir."

"Is this some sort of business for her and her companion?"

He shook his head.

"How did she get into this---this, what do you call this thing?"

"I'm not sure we've given it a name, strange you should ask. She just goes about doing what is asked of her and then she blends in. She doesn't do it for fame or recognition, in fact, she resents the little exposure she does derive. The local newspaper in her town did a story about her coming back to life after she

THE ENDOWMENT

was brought into the hospital DOA. She didn't want any pictures or addresses given. She's not a recluse by any means, but ranchers do have a mundane life, meaning they work hard all day long and then they go to bed early. She has a small fruit ranch in Palisades, where she grows apples, cherries, and a small variety of different other fruit, pears, plums, peaches etc. Delbert and his sister are Grace's neighbors and they are very close. Her father left her enough money to live comfortably and she does not want for anything. Now you know as much about her as I do, Mr. Newberry."

"You mentioned she was generous."

"A while back she was physically abducted and driven to Spokane where she healed a prominent businessman and he handed her a box full of money. She in turn, gave a fair sum of it to a family that needed it to keep from losing their home.

More recently, she helped a four member family escape a tyrant rancher. He paid the guy so little he couldn't afford to live anywhere else, and was forced to live in squalor. They looked like vagrants. She bought the family a home and got him a job in town that would pay him what other mechanics are paid. He was an American Indian with no hope when he happened upon a tent church service - - and Grace.

That man vowed that he would one day help someone in need as Grace helped him. Mr. Newberry, she is just an ordinary woman, picked by God to do his bidding, and that's about all that can be said of it. I must admit she has had some concerns about her place in His plan. It hasn't been a bed of roses for her."

"How can I help her on her quest for serving---God?"

Bob watched Mr. Newberry closely, trying to get a reading as to his sincerity, "Was that a tentative 'God'?"

"Forgive me Mr. Dempsey. God hasn't been in my house or on my lips for years. I suppose as we become more successful, wealthy, we forget about God and what he stands for." He stood and walked to the large window that gave way to the backyard. He watched Gilda as she danced with life in her feet and the joy of becoming whole. Tears welled in his eyes and he reached for a handkerchief from his pocket. He saw his wife on the patio watching Grace and Gilda as they laughed and made small talk. She also was crying as she crossed herself.

"Have you ever seen the movie, '*A Christmas Carol*' Mr. Dempsey? I feel like the old gentleman that is taken around to all the people he has wronged. In my own defense, I don't believe I have wronged people as much as I have forgotten old friends, friends I could have helped. I have become selfishly reclusive, devoid of any personal contact, except with my immediate family. I mean to change all of that now that Miss Jennings has opened my eyes. If you will excuse me I have an errand to run, please don't leave until I come back."

Gilda and Grace came back to the study with Mrs. Newberry at their side. Bob and Delbert were deep in conversation, but stopped as they entered the room.

"Where did R.W. go?" Mrs. Newberry asked.

They looked at each other, who was R.W.?

"Mr. Newberry?"

"R. W. is simpler than Russell Wade, he never liked Russ or Russell, so, it's R.W., Where did he go?"

"He mentioned he had an errand to run. Said he would be right back, and asked us not to leave," Bob responded.

Mrs. Newberry wondered where he could have gone, and how he could have just run out on their guests like that. Oh well, he'll hear about it this evening, she promised herself.

"You folks must be hungry. Could I interest you in some lunch?"

"Oh Grams, could we eat in the patio? Would that be all right with you Grace? There's no wind right now and it's beautiful outside, could we, please?" Gilda pleaded.

The three communicated non-verbally with each other, and in unison nodded their assent. Gilda squealed with delight.

A half hour later the five of them were ready to sit down to lunch on the patio.

"I was hoping your grandfather would be back by now, but we're not going to wait for him. We'll sit down now and Anisia will serve lunch."

"What are we having, Grams?"

"Why, your favorite my dear. Hot dogs and salad."

THE ENDOWMENT

"Oh, Grace!!! Cook makes the best hot dogs ever!!! You'll love them," Gilda gushed. Her demeanor suddenly turned serious and she turned to her grandmother, "Grandmother could I say a prayer before we eat?"

"Why of course honey, that would be nice."

They bowed their heads and waited for Gilda to say her prayer.

"Father in heaven, I want to thank you for sending Grace to make my legs move again. I have always wanted to pray to you but never knew what to say, until now. I think I always knew you would allow me to walk again. I will go to St. Joseph's church from now on if it's all right with Grams, and Father, could you remove the red spot from Grace's face? She's not complaining, but I know she would like that. Amen."

The adults wiped away their tears and Gilda reached for a hot dog, as she softly hummed *Somewhere over the Rainbow*, a happy smile all over her face.

Grace was happy and proud that she had been instrumental in the little girl's recovery. She knew this frail child was special and God must have had his eye on her all the time, considering she and her two associates almost left the Newberry premises. She thought that it almost didn't happen because Grace had become angry. Why was she still susceptible to annoying outbursts that she was sure did not please Him? Why was she so vulnerable to doubt? Doubt nagged at her and made her feel inadequate. She stood and asked for directions to the bathroom, then excused herself and left the table. On her way back to the patio she walked past the kitchen where R.W. stopped her. He was carrying a black leather satchel.

"I'm glad I've caught you alone, Miss Jennings. I don't want my wife to see me giving this to you, even though she would approve. Mr. Dempsey informed me of your past endeavors and I wish to offer you this money to assist you in all your future undertakings where ever they may take you. Your boss is highly respected. I'm not trying to buy my way into heaven, just trying to assist his earthly disciple to help those less fortunate. My family will not miss this money and you could put it to better use than I have. I would like to suggest you place this satchel in your car and say nothing to my family. I assure you

170

this would meet with their approval as you can readily see from the love you have given to our little Gilda. I have never seen someone so alive or so grateful. She wants to be a physician someday and I believe she will be. She has been to the best doctors and the best hospitals to no avail, and you have, in minutes, changed her life forever. I have inserted my business card in the bag. If you should need my assistance in any way, I am at your service. Apparently, my facial features do resemble the great eagle or was that your reference in calling me an eagle when you became angry with me and departed?" He grinned.

She blushed, "I'm sorry I said that sir, I am usually in better control. Maybe it was the long trip over here or that I didn't sleep well last night, at any rate, I apologize. You didn't deserve that abuse, sir."

"Quite the contrary, Miss Jennings, I did deserve your ire, but thank you." He extended the valise to her and she turned, walked down the hall and out the front door to the car.

Grace met Bob and Delbert at the front door and the Newberry's were just behind them. It was getting late and the three still had to drive over the pass before nightfall.

"Promise me you will call me sometime. Please Grace," Gilda pleaded as she hugged her closely.

"I promise," she said, her eyes welling.

"I don't even know where you live. Is it far?"

"It's over the Cascade Mountains, a drive through Snoqualmie Pass, to a small town by the name of Palisades."

"I've never heard of Palisades."

"Few people have."

Bob and Delbert walked to the car, Grace gave one final hug to Gilda and smiled at R.W. and Mary then turned to the car and they drove away. This time the gate was open.

THE ENDOWMENT

CHAPTER 55

Delbert and Bob had just pulled into the strip center shopping center parking lot and were looking for Grace's blue and white Buick sedan when they saw two men talking to her by her car. From the distance the scene looked ominous as the two men kept looking around, as they escorted her to their light truck.

Delbert had stopped to allow an older couple to walk in front of the car. Both had canes and were moving slowly.

"Bob, can you see what's happening over there?"

"They appear to be walking her to the next row of cars. Do you recognize either of them, Delbert?"

"Too far away."

"Maybe she knows them."

"Maybe, but my gut tells me otherwise?" Again, he had to wait for pedestrian to walk across in front of them.

"I'm not certain, but I think the truck they got into is leaving the lot."

"Keep an eye on it Bob and see which way it turns," the depth of his concern was clear in his voice.

Finally, the lane was clear but Delbert still had to drive slowly for fear of hitting the shoppers, who seemed to be everywhere.

"Are you sure she got into that truck?"

"Delbert, I'm not positive, but I didn't see any other vehicle leave." They reached the exit of the parking lot.

"Go right."

Delbert squealed the tires as he made a right on Miller, and began speeding up the long street.

"I think I see the truck up ahead, not sure, but its at least five cars up. Do you see it Delbert?"

"I do. Do you think we should stop and call the cops?"

"I was thinking the same thing, but if we stop, we might lose her. Beside, I don't know if there's a phone booth on Miller Street."

"They're turning right on Cherry. Can you make out if she is in that truck?" Delbert asked anxiously.

"Can't tell."

172

"Oh my God, what if we're following the wrong truck?"

Delbert was getting overwrought and started to lose it...panic.

"I'm going to close the gap and see if she's really in that truck, and if she is, I'm going to ram it and hope for the best."

"Delbert, I'm all for getting closer to verify she is in the truck, but I don't think you ought to ram it."

He drove up to within one car length of the truck.

"I think I see three heads," Delbert said, fear straining his voice.

"I think we're following the right truck," Bob said. "God, please let us be following the right truck."

At Western Avenue the truck turned left.

"There headed up the Canyon Road. I don't like that. There is only a few houses up there and it's pretty desolate."

"You better hang back a little, Del, or they're going to realize we're following them."

"Come to think of it, this the only way in or out," Delbert grinned.

"There's a house up on that little knoll. Maybe we could ask to use their phone. Go ahead and park at the entrance of this driveway and I'll walk up to the house. If you see the truck coming back down, blow the horn three times and I'll come running."

Delbert kept his eyes peeled on the road and after about one minute, Bob came jogging down the driveway.

"Nobody home, dam it."

They drove up the dirt road looking for the truck and saw another lonely home at the side of the dusty lane. He drove to the side of the route and stopped.

"Be back in a few." Bob said jumping out of the car.

Three minutes later he came trotting out of the house.

"Good news and bad news. Bad news the old man in there doesn't have a phone. The good news, he told me the people that own the truck we followed live just around the next bend. Their last name is Judd. He doesn't like them, says they're religious zealots or just plain crazy. He believes there is four or five in the family. It's the next house up on the right."

"What do you think?" Delbert asked looking up the dirt road.

"Well, if we go up there, we would be trespassing and the old man said they're crazy."

"What would you call someone abducting a woman from a shopping center?"

"Let's go up there." Bob said with determination.

The two drove up and parked beside the pickup they had followed up the canyon road. They stared at the house, waiting to see if anyone saw them drive up.

"See any movement in the house?" Delbert asked quietly.

Bob shook his head.

The two stepped from the car and began walking deliberately to the front door.

CHAPTER 56

A man stepped out of the front door with a shotgun in his arms.

"What's your business here?" he said pointing a 12 gauge at the two men.

"We believe you have a friend of ours in your home." Delbert said aggressively.

The man gazed at the two men and then another younger man stepped out with a 30 Caliber rifle.

"We're not leaving without her and you better not have hurt her." Delbert threatened.

"I believe you're trespassing, wouldn't you agree?" The man said arrogantly.

"We don't believe Grace Jennings came up here on her own free will." Bob said candidly.

"We think she did."

"Let her tell us that." Delbert provoked.

The man with the shotgun walked into the house and came back to the door with Grace at his side.

"William, Tom, the Judd's are friends of mine and we're just having a conversation about God. I'm all right, go on home, I'll be all right."

Delbert and Bob stood for a few seconds and glared at the Judd's and then turned and walked back to their car and drove away.

The two drove in silence until they reached Western Avenue.

"So what are we going to do now, William?" Delbert said with a grin on his face.

"Well, the right thing to do would be to go to the Police Station and report this." Bob said earnestly. "Pull over to the side of the street and let's think about this. I know you don't want to leave the area, nor do I. So what do you think about me using someone's phone around here and calling the cops on the Judds."

"Sounds like a good plan, let me turn around and face the Canyon Road so they don't sneak out."

THE ENDOWMENT

Bob trotted off to the nearest home and was back in about ten minutes.

"They're going to send Detective Kelli Finnigan up here in about an hour, the other Detective would be longer, so we'll just have to bide our time here."

"You're kidding, one hour?"

"They didn't think it was urgent."

"It will be dark in an hour."

"I think that's the truck coming our direction."

They both concentrated on the truck as it turned down Cherry Street with only the driver in the cab. Delbert turned the engine off and they both stared ahead. They discussed the possibility of driving up under the shield of darkness and parking at the old man's house that told them the Judd's were crazy. They would stealthily approach and observe the house and when the opportunity presented itself they would over take the man with the shotgun and rescue Grace.

An hour later, "Wow, when it gets dark up here, it gets dark." Bob said looking up the direction of the canyon. "I think I've got a flashlight in the glove box."

" Do you think there are any rattlesnakes out here?" Bob asked timidly.

"We're going to stay on the beaten path and I've got my trusty light."

The duo walked up the road without talking and then turned into the driveway until they were about forty yards from the house. They stopped by a large thistle bush and observed the house.

"Did you see a dog when we were here earlier?" Delbert whispered.

"No."

They crept along the side of the road until they were only about ten yards from the house. They hid behind a young Douglas pine.

The door opened and the man that had held the shotgun looked down the road. " I don't see no lights yet, guess he may not come back tonight." He said to the occupants of the house. He was not holding a shotgun now and then walked back inside.

176

"If the old man was right there should only be four people inside that house. How do you read it?" Delbert whispered.

Bob agreed quietly. They discussed a brief plan for breaking into the house and rescuing Grace. Delbert would go in first and overcome the man. Bob would find and control the shotgun. They checked the road behind them for headlights and the return of the truck. Bob touched Delbert shoulder and whispered. "When ever you're ready." Bob nodded. They stood and crept up to the front door.

CHAPTER 57

Delbert tried the doorknob as quietly as he could and when it didn't turn, he stepped back, lowered his shoulder and crashed through it. Delbert and Bob assessed the situation quickly.

The man stood and rushed to the wall where the shotgun was leaning. Delbert cut him off and threw a right hand that connected squarely on the man's jaw. He crumpled to the floor and remained motionless. The other three were a young girl and two older women.

"Where's Grace?" Delbert demanded.

The young girl pointed toward a room.

Bob stood, shotgun in hand and told the women to huddle together and Delbert rushed to the door and opened it to a tied up Grace on a wooden chair.

"You all right Grace?"

"I'm fine."

"Did they hurt you?"

"No, they weren't as bad as you might think. They think I'm one of the devil's disciples. They saw me at Heavens Gate Tent Revival Church." She said as Delbert pulled on the simple shoe knot and unwound the rope from Grace's body. She hugged Delbert hard and kissed him on the cheek. "I knew my guardian angel would be coming for me, so I was never too worried. I think they were considering, and now the word eludes me. It means taking the devil out of me." "Exorcism?"

"That's the word."

They walked out to where Bob was holding the women huddled together. The man on the floor groaned and Delbert walked over to him and leaned down.

"You all right?"

"Feel like a horse kicked me." The man said rubbing his chin. Delbert helped him stand.

"I'm sorry, but you did point a 12 gauge at us."

"My mistake. It didn't have any shells in the chamber though."

Delbert retrieved a chair for the man and sat him down.

178

"We're Christians, you know," the older woman said looking straight ahead.

Grace walked to the woman and stood directly in front of her. She peered into her eyes then passed her hand across her face.

"Are you blind?"

The woman grimaced and tears ran down her face. She bit her upper lip and the younger adult placed a handkerchief in her hand.

"She can't see," the little girl spoke, "she's been blind since she was born."

The room became quiet and Grace remained gazing at the blind woman. She reached out and took the woman's hand and pulled her gently toward the room Grace had been imprisoned in.

"Where are you taking my wife?"

"Sir, I assure you Grace will do nothing to your wife she would regret." Delbert said pulling a chair from the kitchen and sitting down beside the man.

The door closed and the house became still, no one said anything.

Five minutes passed. Nothing.

Ten minutes passed. Nothing.

Then there was movement in the room and again silence. There were voices heard almost as murmurs and the door opened.

"Thomas Judd, this woman is not the devil's disciple any more than I am. I can see, and it's not the devils doing. It's God will. She belongs to God," she hugged her husband and kissed him.

She turned and looked down at little Betty. "Honey, you're more beautiful than I would have guessed," and she hugged her warmly.

"Giselle, you couldn't be more attractive and it goes with your generous personality. I love you so."

Grace I don't how to thank you and at the same time ask for your forgiveness for me and my family for what we did to you, but I hope you will find it in your heart to forgive us."

THE ENDOWMENT

Grace walked over and hugged Wilma and then turned and faced Thomas Judd and hugged him too.

"I'm a little tired, I hope you don't mind that I'd like to go home. It's been a long day, but I'm glad I got to meet all of you."

Giselle and Betty rushed to Grace and hugged her tightly as tears of joy cascaded down their cheeks.

The three exited into the dark night with nothing but a wayward light showing the way to their car.

CHAPTER 58

Grace and Delbert were heading back from a Sunday outing at Lake Chelan. The sun was just now setting, and they decided to take the 25 Mile Creek Road that comes out in Entiat, merges with highway 97 and can be followed to Palisades. This road was less traveled and it was a nice change for meandering back to their homes. Delbert was driving his 1948 Buick Super 8, the car he loved and pampered.

They were each mentally rehashing the day, as was their custom. Both were quiet people and comfortable with the silence.

Grace was thinking about the way things were going and that her life was flowing somewhat evenly with her endowment and it was a strange thought. Sometimes she felt so special with her gift from God. Other times she was so confused. Recently, she learned not to think about it so intensely or the doubts would creep in. Funny, Delbert just took it all in stride. Just went along with everything she did...or didn't do. In a lot of ways she really did not know this man, her protector. She liked him a lot, maybe even loved him. Every once in a while she wondered if *he* was able to love someone. She was aware he liked her and June had practically said he loved Grace. But was she just using the term, love, loosely?

"There's a car behind us that has slowed down when we slow down, and then falls behind and then catches up to us. I don't think it's following us but I don't like the way it's behaving."

Grace turned around but all she could see were the headlights of the car. She didn't say anything because Delbert was not concerned. The drive continued this way for a few more miles until the car drove around Delbert and quickly sped out of sight.

"What was the model of the car?" Grace asked.

"I believe it was a Lincoln, fifty five or six."

"Could you see the driver?"

THE ENDOWMENT

"Looked like two men in the front. Never noticed the back seat, but it could have been another man. Glad they went around us."

They had driven another five or six miles when they came upon a car, with the hood up, blocking the lane they were driving in.

Delbert slowed as they approached.

"Some kind of car problem?" Grace wondered.

"Maybe. Looks like the car that went around us back there. Yep, it's the Lincoln," Delbert said as they approached.

"I don't see anybody around the car. The passenger door is open. Can you see anyone?" Grace asked, as she strained to see. The car's lights were on, but no one in sight.

"I don't know Grace, something doesn't look right here. What do you think, should we stop and see, or keep going?"

"What if it's some kind of health issue, maybe a heart attack or accident? Maybe I could be of some service. Go ahead and pull over behind the car."

Delbert blew his horn. Nothing. He blinked his headlights.

"I'm going to walk up to the car and see if there's anybody in there. Grace, lock your door and when I get out, slide over to the driver's side. If it's some kind of trick, you drive off. Understand? Keep the engine running, and I'm going to lock the door behind me."

Delbert stepped out and listened for any sounds coming from the car. All he heard were the crickets on the side of the road and his car's engine humming. He took in a deep breath and walked directly to the open door on the passenger side and looked into the front seat. A man was lying on the seat, he had a pistol pointed directly at Delbert.

He turned to warn Grace but there were already two men at the driver's side of his car. She had turned the engine off and was getting out. The man in the Lincoln stepped out of the car and ordered the other men to bring the woman to him. Delbert tensed and was on the verge of making a break toward Grace, but the gun suddenly poked hard into his ribs, held him in check.

Grace was brought to the Lincoln, and hoods were pulled roughly over both their heads, their hands were tied. A gravely

182

voice warned them that if they tried to pull the hoods off they would die.

"Are you all right Grace?" Delbert asked quietly.

"I'm fine, and you?"

"I'm OK."

The drive remained quiet. The men did not speak even to each other.

"I don't suppose you could tell us where you're taking us?" Delbert asked with angst in his voice.

The car they were riding in eventually turned off the highway on to a dirt road. The driver slowed because of the rough terrain. They were ascending and the road was winding. Occasionally, the bottom of the car would hit a high spot on the middle of the road. Finally, the car stopped and the men pulled Grace and Delbert from the car.

It was an old log cabin, with a pine front door with two glassless windows on each side. The windows had shutters that could be pulled closed from inside by a leather thong. Crudely assembled, they did keep out the elements.

Delbert was brought in and thrown on the wooden floor. He listened for Grace's entrance. After a few minutes, he heard the sounds of someone manhandling her and she was deposited at the other end of the room.

"Grace!"

"I'm here, Delbert."

The room got quiet.

Delbert thought he had only heard the sounds of two men. He wondered about the other two. Delbert tried to sit up.

The door opened and one of the men came into the room. He dropped something on the floor not too far from where he was lying. He tried to think what the sounds were. The man approached him and turned him on his back and tied his legs. The other man came in and dropped some more of the same sound. He smelled Sagebrush. That was the sound, Sagebrush. Why would they bring Sagebrush into the room? The room got quiet again. He thought he heard the sound of the car's engine. They must be leaving, he thought. The door opened and one of the men walked in and stood where the Sagebrush had been dropped. He heard the sound of a container with liquid sloshing

183

around. Delbert smelled Kerosene and then he heard the crackling of fire on the Sagebrush.

"I hope you burn in Hell, you cowards," Grace shouted at the man that had started the fire.

The door slammed close and the room was quiet except for the crackle of the flames.

CHAPTER 59

"I'm sorry Delbert," she sobbed.

"My legs are tied Grace and I can't move," he yelled. "If I could just get this hood off I could see which way to roll."

Grace rolled to one side and bumped her head against a log wall. She thought she might have moved to a corner of the cabin and decided to roll back. When she did, the hood caught on something and was pulled away from her head. She could see the flames from the Sagebrush in the middle of the cabin. She looked around for Delbert.

"Delbert, my hood fell off, but I can't see you."

He made an attempt to roll so she could find him.

She had been able to keep her legs apart just a little when the men were tying them and now the rope was loose on her legs. She inched herself to the log wall and then rolled on her back, raised herself up to a sitting position and leaned against the wall. She rocked until she had her weight on her feet and stood. Grace hopped a few inches and fell.

"Damn," she uttered, then raised herself to a sitting position and laboriously scooted herself like an inchworm over to Delbert. She began assessing how to untie him.

"I think the fire's dying out Delbert," she noted.

"Thank God, I hope it is," he responded. " Are you close to me?"

"I'm by your feet."

"I think we should try and untie my hand's first. Don't you think?"

"Yes." She scooted up to where she thought his hands were. She searched with her fingers until she touched a part of his body.

"That's the back of my leg. You need to come up just a little more."

She inched herself up and looked around to see if she could see his hands. The fire was giving off less light. The cabin was getting darker. She moved so close she was touching his fingers with hers. Grace moved her arms up and felt the rope around Delbert's hands and looked for the tie knot. She found it

THE ENDOWMENT

and began pulling to no avail; she pulled on a different one, again no help. Then another, and this one began to unravel.

Delbert felt the ropes loosen on his wrists. They were free. He brought his hands to his head and took the hood off and looked around. The fire *was* dying out. He untied his feet, and then Grace's hands. She freed her feet and Delbert helped her to stand. He picked up a burning limb and walked slowly around the small cabin trying to assess the contents. In the corner there appeared to be a wooden frame that could be a bed and a small metal stove. They moved slowly toward the door and opened it.

Outside, it was overcast and they were unable to see any stars or Moon. It was totally dark. They shuffled back inside where the fire was slowly going out. Delbert picked up some of the sagebrush and held it over the little bit of flame and tried to keep the fire going. As it started to burn he gathered the other limbs that had not burned.

"I think we should stay in the cabin tonight."

Grace agreed and they moved to one side of the cabin and sat, backs against the wall, watching the flames of the small fire.

Delbert woke in the morning to the scolding of a Blue Jay outside the cabin and found Grace with her head against his shoulder. He could see some daylight through the partially shuttered windows. He wanted to move but was afraid to wake Grace. He had tilted, slightly to one side during the night and now wanted to right himself, so he moved ever so slightly and woke up Grace. The fire had gone out.

"I see some blue out there," he whispered.

Delbert stood and helped Grace stand. They were stiff and cold. They walked outside to a crisp, bright morning. Delbert could see a sparsely used dirt road leading to the cabin.

"I guess we'd better start hiking."

Delbert nodded.

They were walking down the road in a descending mode, which is what Delbert had guessed from the night before. As they hiked, Grace's hand touched Delbert's.

"How come your hand is warm? Mine are freezing."

He just smiled at her.

"Could I hold your hand?"

186

He blushed. "Sure."

She reached out and took his hand. It was nice.

He felt his heart take a couple of extra beats.

Sweet Delbert, he's always there for me, always, she thought. That was the reason Delbert was so special to her, but he was more than that. She looked up at the wonderful man and beamed as he kept his head straight away down the road. They had marched down the winding dirt road for two miles or so when they came upon a smoldering car against a large Douglas Fur tree and it too, was partially burned. The car appeared to have been black. Delbert approached it and could still feel the heat from the charred rubber tires. He could see the remains of two charred bodies in the front seat.

"I believe this is two of our captors," Delbert said sadly.

"Oh my God!" Grace shouted.

CHAPTER 60

"Do you really believe the reason you were abducted by those men was to kill you?" Bob Dempsey asked.

Grace nodded.

"And that you had wished for the fire, those men had started in the log cabin, to go out. Do you feel responsible for those men who burned up in their car? That it was some kind of avenging thing directed from God?"

Again she nodded.

"Tell me again exactly what you said, when the men started the fire in the log cabin."

She stood and walked to her kitchen window and looked out at the barn and the corral.

"I shouted, *I hope you burn in Hell.*"

Bob turned his attention to Delbert. He made eye contact and then looked away.

"What about the Deputy Sheriff and Detective Finnigan? They were sure it was a mechanical malfunction. They had the best mechanics checking the Lincoln. All three of them agreed the car had hit bottom on the rough road several times and one of those times it had broken the brake lines. That car had no brakes when it hit that tree. You can look at the brake lines and see they were damaged," Bob argued. He could see he was not making any headway. He was almost sure she was in need of a psychiatrist. He had called Detective Finnigan and asked for a recommendation.

Finnigan had mentioned the department used at least three different shrinks. All good psychiatrists, however, she had seen what Angie Lansing had done with the young lady from the college that had been a witness to a recent murder in Wenatchee. She recommended Dr. Lansing and gave him Lansing's number.

188

CHAPTER 61

It had been almost a month since they had escaped from the cabin in the hills around Chelan. She had been listless, not much like herself. She liked Bob Dempsey and had a lot of respect for the man, and didn't want anything bad to happen to him. Delbert was special, she now believed she loved him, whatever love is. There was definitely something she felt in her bones for the wonderful, gentle, quiet man. She was sure it was love. For that reason alone she could not pursue the path she was on. How could she go on living if another unfortunate situation happened and he was killed? She knew she couldn't and didn't even want to give it consideration.

Grace had looked and found the lady that used to give Bibles away on the street corner. She had found the perfect lady to give all the money they had accrued. She was the Mother Teresa of Wenatchee and Grace felt she would do justice to all the money.

Shirley Ullenkamp had said, "She had God's eye for those who were in need. Her own eyes could be deceived, but not "God's eye." Grace had felt a certain relief after her brief but assuring conversation with Shirley. The story she gave the bank where she opened her 'God's Account,' was, she had inherited the money from a woman who had worked directly with God. If they had any questions, they could take it up with Him. The bank was happy to receive the money. The Vice President had smiled politely and deposited the money eagerly. The lady with the tattered attire, hawking Bibles had become credible. She would champion those who were in need. She was truly God's disciple. Grace smiled as she thought about Shirley Ullenkamp. She looked over at Delbert who was just sitting, watching her.

"I was thinking of the Bible lady, Shirley Ullenkamp. There are a lot of wonderful people in this world and we've been fortunate to meet some of them."

The man in her life nodded.

CHAPTER 62

Grace Jennings invited Delbert to come over so she could tell him she had received a call from a lady in Pateros, Washington. She was willing to go for one more 'case.' She felt it was important to help this young girl with polio, who was confined to a wheel chair. It would be only the two of them going to the small town on the other side of Chelan,

Tom Dempsey had gone back to Seattle and his job at the Seattle Times.

She had called to have a new telephone number. No one would have access to her new number because it would not be listed.

Grace had fixed a nice lunch for her and Delbert. She was enthused about going to Pateros only because it was the final time.

Delbert could see the renewed Grace. She was happy again instead of depressed and quiet. It really was all about her and what she should do. There was a lot of pressure with her gift. She had expressed her reasons for stopping the healings and trying to remain anonymous. He had always accepted her wishes. If she wanted to disengage herself from the path she was walking, he would support her. He would never challenge her decisions. Now she was happy and that's all he could want for her.

Tomorrow they would drive to Pateros and she would apply her gift once again and then it would be the end. She would fade into a normal, regular life and become an orchardist again.

"Do you think June would object to you staying with me tonight and we can get an early start tomorrow?" Grace asked quietly.

"I'll let her know and be right back," he said as he walked out the front door.

Grace sighed as she watched Delbert stroll up the road to his home. She felt good about what she was doing. Finally,

190

resolve. She would become a dedicated farmer again. She stood by the open door and heard one of her two horses whinney. Grace strolled to the corral and her beautiful Appaloosa, Painted Cloud by the Nez Perce Indian who had sold her the horse. She had bought the horse in Palouse Country.

Over time the words 'a' and 'Palouse' (the word for horse in the Sehaptin language) were merged to form the word Appaloosa. Painted Cloud was hard to describe, she was either all white with black blotches or she was all black with white blotches.

Her other horse was a chestnut Paso Fino mare, with four white stockings and a white blaze on her beautiful face, Donita Minda was fourteen hands tall and well proportioned, and was a beautiful horse.

Grace walked to the gate where they could put their heads over the top. She wiped the tears from her eyes and looked at her beautiful horses. She touched their faces and smiled with tears rolling down her face.

"You've missed them, haven't you?" Delbert said quietly standing beside her.

"I have, I didn't realize how much until now. Delbert would you help with the tack?" "Would you mind riding Painted Cloud?" she asked as she opened the barn door.

"I've always wanted to ride that horse, it would be my pleasure. She's a beauty."

They rode for about two hours along the small trails surrounding the mountains of Palisades.

They returned and stabled the horses, had a light dinner and were enjoying coffee with a piece of Grace's home made apple pie.

"You know, I think we sometimes forget the simple things of life. I think I took the ride along the mountain for granted. Would you say you're a home body, Delbert?"

He nodded, mouth stuffed full of pie.

"I don't think you've ever disagreed with me, Mr. Blair and I want to know why," she challenged.

He shook his head.

"Do you like me, Delbert? I mean, I know you like me, but do you really like me...do you?" She was embarrassed,

THE ENDOWMENT

didn't know what to do now so she jumped up and asked, "Would you like another piece of pie?"

He nodded again. "Yes and yes."

"You mean yes for another piece of pie and yes for, do you?"

"Yes," and he nodded.

"Well." she said and sat down at the kitchen table and stared at the pie. Daisy came over, sat at her feet and looked up at Grace with her soulful eyes.

"Did you hear that Daisy? He said yes and yes"

Daisy stood in front of Grace, wagged her little stubby tail and gave one short bark.

"Delbert did you hear that, Daisy and Mandy never bark unless there's a problem. So what's the problem, Daisy? You don't like Delbert?" Daisy walked to the other end of the kitchen and lay down beside Mandy.

"Would 5:00 AM be too early to drive to Pateros in the morning?" She asked changing the subject.

He nodded and she smiled.

" Well, you can sleep in the guest room. If you don't mind the dogs, they start out in that room and then end up at the foot of my bed in the morning. So you would have to leave the door open."

Delbert walked into the bedroom and sat at the edge of the double bed. He really wasn't sleepy, but he knew if he lay down he would fall asleep. Grace's bedroom was at the other end of the hallway, so it wasn't necessary to close the door to undress and get into bed. He could hear Grace talking to Daisy and Mandy. The two dogs walked up to the door, looked in, walked up to the side of the bed and peered at Delbert. They turned and left the room, probably headed back to Grace's room.

He lay with his hands behind his head, thinking about what Grace had said earlier. He wanted to tell Grace how much he loved her, but just didn't have the guts to do it. He thought he had been lying there for hours until he looked at the clock and saw it had only been seven minutes. He turned the light off and stared at the dark ceiling, turned the light back on and stepped into his pants. He walked quietly to Grace's open bedroom door and stood looking in.

192

"Did you need something Delbert?"

He cleared his throat. Grace turned her bedside lamp on. The two dogs raised their heads from the floor at the end of the bed and gazed at Delbert in the doorway.

"I did…I did want to say something Grace, but now that I'm here, it seems silly. I'm sorry, I hope I didn't wake you."

"I was awake."

"OK, well, good night." And Delbert walked quickly back to his bedroom.

CHAPTER 63

Four and one half hours later.

The intruder looked at his watch, it was 2:30 and he knew she had been asleep for hours. Most ranchers were early birds. He knew she lived alone. He slipped the file into the lock and the doorjamb and the door opened easily. Inside the dogs both raised their heads and listened. The prowler walked using his small pen lamp avoiding the furniture. The door was open to the bedroom on the right. He stopped and listened. There was the soft sound of breathing. He turned off the pen light, crept in and stood beside the bed. He pulled the pistol from his coat pocket and aimed for the torso. He fired two quick rounds into her body and turned to the door. He rushed out of the bedroom, toward the front entrance. Suddenly he felt something heavy hit his back, and a tearing sensation in his right shoulder. He yelled out in pain as he fell against the large chair he had seen on the way in. His head hit a wooden oak stand and he landed on his back. The dog hadn't made a sound but the intruder could smell its breath close to his face. The dog bit into his chest trying to find his neck. The interloper screamed and tried to reach for his pistol. It had fallen on the floor somewhere. A light went on.

"Back Daisy, back." Grace ordered. She stood with a black .45 pistol in her hand. It was pointed at the trespasser. Daisy crouched, her face inches from the man's face, still snarling and waiting for the next command.

"Move an inch and she'll tear your throat out," Grace shouted. Mandy was standing on the other side of the man now, looking as vicious as Daisy. The man was bleeding from the open wound on his chest and three paw scratches on his right cheek. Grace picked up the pistol with a white handkerchief and placed it on the kitchen table.

"Delbert!" Grace shouted. "Delbert can you hear me?"

Grace rushed to the telephone that was in the kitchen. She dialed 0.

"Operator."

"Get me the Police."

"Is this an emergency?"

"Yes."

"Police department."

"I think there has been a shooting and I have the prowler in my front room."

"What's your name ma'am and where do you live?"

Grace gave the policeman the information and waited for their arrival.

June Blair walked into the front room and stared in horror at the scenario.

"June would you go check on Delbert? He's in the bedroom on the right?"

She rushed toward the bedroom and a few seconds later she began wailing from the room, "Oh my God Grace, I think Delbert's dead."

June walked out of the bedroom just as Detective Kelli Finnigan walked into the front room.

THE ENDOWMENT

CHAPTER 64

It was a small gathering at Wenatchee City Cemetery. There was Grace and June and George Campos, the Kuckles ranch foreman, Jimmy Marr, Grace's foreman, Colt Hobson, the deputy sheriff, Detective Kelli Finnigan, and Janice Maybelle Jackson who now lived in Seattle had heard about the accident and called Grace.

The small group stood quietly in the middle of the green burial ground. Grace was cried out and just stared at the casket that held Delbert's body.

Janice Maybelle Jackson had just finished singing Ave Maria and sang Taps.

Everyone was choked up, and tears ran freely as they heard Jackson's beautiful soprano voice. Grace looked up at the sky when she felt the raindrops fall on her head. She unfurled her umbrella and motioned for the man to lower the box.

"Are you sure you don't want to come over to the house for a while, Grace.

"Thank you June, I think I want to be alone for a while."

She thanked the mourners for attending the funeral before they disbursed. June was still talking to Janice when Grace hurried to her car. She drove out of the cemetery fighting tears, but knew she couldn't cry, not now, not with the rain and the windshield wipers banging from side to side.

Thirty minutes later she walked into her front room. Daisy and Mandy came to her as if they knew she was in need of consolation. She hung her coat and umbrella and sat at the kitchen table. She turned the small radio on, stood and walked to the sink. She poured out the little bit of coffee and rinsed the pot. The radio was interfering with her thoughts. She turned it off. She made two cups of coffee and sat, waiting for it to brew. Her head bent, hands on her lap, she began to cry out loud.

The dogs had approached their master and licked her hands. She looked up and still crying, began to laugh. They looked up at her face, almost with sadness in their sweet fuzzy faces.

196

"Oh my God, you're feeling sorry for me, aren't you?" she said, crying uncontrollably.

She knelt down on both knees and put her arms around each dog. She wept. She loved her animals, and they loved her no matter what she did. The dogs lay down beside her and just gazed at their grieving mentor.

" Why God, why?" she shouted.

THE ENDOWMENT

CHAPTER 64

Three years later in Taos, New Mexico.

The Police Chief and his only officer, a Sergeant, were walking to their car when the Sergeant stopped his boss.

"Who's the lady on that beautiful Appaloosa?" he pointed to the woman riding out of town trailed by two dogs.

"Don't know much about her, she moved on the North end of Taos about three years ago. She bought the old LeDoux ranch; has a couple of horses, some sheep and goats and those two dogs." The Chief responded. She's not very friendly, but then again, she doesn't make any trouble."

"Saw her in one of the small trinket shops the other day. She's pretty, even with the mark on her face," the Sergeant added.

Grace rode out of Taos on her way to a home on the north side of Taos. She had moped, read and cleaned, built a small corral adjacent to the larger one. She had built a porch over the backdoor of her new 'old' home. Now, here she was, riding to help someone again and she didn't know why.

CHAPTER 65

Tom Dempsey had been able to locate the whereabouts of Grace Jennings from June Blair. But he was never to contact or make known where she was to any one. He agreed and then subscribed to a Taos, New Mexico bi-weekly paper called the *Horse Fly*. The article that caught Tom's eye was written by one of the staff writers.

"Alejandro, the youngest son of the Richard and Penelope Garcia family, who had been wheel chair bound since birth, was suddenly healed and is now doing chores around the house. The family would only state that it was a miracle. They had no idea how the miracle came about."

Tom laid the paper down and walked out the door.

He nodded and smiled happily as he strode to his car.

Also by Joseph Montoya via Amazon.com:

The Shade
Where is Brian Douglas?
The Innocent
Mysterious Ways

Made in the USA
Charleston, SC
27 August 2013